THE PELEG
PALADINS
Book two
CHRONICLES

Matthew Christian Harding

PALADINS

Zoe and Sozo Publishing
3034 Millers Landing Rd.
Gloucester, Virginia 23061

www.MatthewChristianHarding.com

Cover Design by Zoe and Sozo Publishing

All scripture references are from the King James Version of the Bible.

ISBN 978-0-9823484-1-3

Praise for *The Peleg Chronicles*

"The unique strength of this book is its faithful, biblical contextualization, combined with powerfully fun creativity. The stout faith of men and women who, through great adventures, endure hardship for the sake of their God will inspire you and your children ... The book is a great family read-aloud that you will not want to put down - our family didn't. In fact, my children continually reminded me to get back to the story so we could find out what happened to Lord McDougal, Fergus Leatherhead, and the foundlings."
— **Steve Murphy**, Publisher, *Homeschooling Today Magazine*

"Harding blends a thriving feudal society complete with knights, counts, and princesses with the dragons (think dinosaurs), giants, and a cave-dwelling group of men called dwarves with the ongoing attempts of darkness to smother the light. Perhaps the fastest way I can describe it is to say that Foundlings is something akin to Lord of the Rings meets biblical fiction, with no magic, evolution, or humanism thrown into the mix ... It's rare to find an author so dedicated to folding biblical truth within the pages of a good, clean story that honors God and promotes Godly character. Harding left us with a dramatic cliffhanger at *Foundling's* end, and our entire family is now eagerly awaiting a new set of adventures for Lord McDougal and his band of motley, faithful comrades."
— **Jennifer Bogart**, www.Quiverfullfamily.com

"I enjoyed reading *Foundlings*. Some parts were action-packed while all parts were written with details that stir up the imagination. I especially appreciated the way you tied in Biblical messages throughout the story. I think a lot of folks will like your writing style."
— **Russ Miller,**
Founder of *Creation, Evolution & Science Ministries*
www.creationministries.org

"This is an exciting Christian alternative to novels with wizards, witches, and magic. I am pleased to offer my boys a book that will satisfy their fascination with dragons as well as help them visualize the power of God. Reading God's Word throughout the novel is just another way to help them absorb it in their hearts. I would certainly recommend this book, especially to families with teen to young adult boys. I look forward to gathering the other books in the series as they are released so I can find out what happens!"
— **Krystin Corneilson,** *The Old Schoolhouse Magazine*

"My wife Andrea has already finished it and loved it…very hard to put down. But she wasn't happy when it ended…SHE WANTED MORE! — **Chris**

"5 out of 5 Stars! Great book for kids and their parents. We just finished this book reading to our 8, 6, and 4 year old and they loved it. One good sign that a book is well written is that the parents enjoy reading it as well and this book meets that re-quirement. Good character development with real heroes that you would want your children to emulate. Scripture was inter-woven throughout the story but we loved that it didn't seem forced or unnatural. So glad we found this book. Can't wait for Book 2. It left us hanging at the end!
— Amazon review by **Christy** (PA United States)

"I loved it! It truly was my all time favorite book I have ever read. I cannot wait until you release the second one."
— **Chad**, age 13

"This book was totally AWESOME! I liked how loyal Lord McDougal is to his God, and his friends. "The Gospel" at the end of the book is great for those who are just learning about God, and those who need to know more about Him. This book will be handed down in my family for generations!"
— **Rachel**, age 12

Table of Contents

I.	Correspondence	13
II.	Pip	19
III.	Staffsmitten	24
IV.	Hunt-Fest	28
V.	A Plan	33
VI.	Strongbow	41
VII.	Hyenae	48
VIII.	A Cup of Tea	55
IX.	Ambush	62
X.	A Terrible Blow	67
XI.	Lunace, Ogre, and Goblin	75
XII.	Buried	83
XIII.	Grave Robbers	90
XIV.	The Interview	106
XV.	The Test	119
XVI.	Distressed	130
XVII.	A Home of Sorts	140
XVIII.	Dinner Party	147
XIX.	The Chronicler's Ship	156

XX.	The Verdict	163
XXI.	Fergus Unsure	169
XXII.	Fergus Pulled In	183
XXIII.	The Rules of Engagement	189
XXIV.	Flummery Gate	196
XXV.	The Oracles	205
XXVI.	Crack Brained Crazy	212
XXVII.	Combat of Honor	224
XXVIII.	Death Comes Quickly	233
XXIX.	Gimcrack's Search	238
XXX.	Giants	246

— Dragons and Dinosaurs —

— Giants —

LIST OF CHARACTERS

Thiery- *foundling, aspiring ranger and beast-master.*
Suzie- *foundling, adopted sister of Thiery.*

Oded- *son of a giant, slow witted, gentle but capable warrior; ranger and beast-master; guardian of Thiery and Suzie.*
Ubaldo- *Oded's deaf twin; ranger and beast-master.*

Count Rosencross- *hungry for power and personal glory, yet an awakening conscience plagues him.*
The Priest- *the Count's personal Dragon Priest; tried to sacrifice his son, Thiery, to his false god.*

The Chronicler- *Master of the Citadel; over 200 years old, lived in Babel before the dispersion.*
Diego Dandolo- *the Chronicler's assistant, former sneak.*

Staffsmitten- *honorary non-dwarf member of the Dwarven Brotherhood, lesser gate-keeper, naturalist, friend of Gimcrack.*
Gimcrack- *map-maker, inventor, dwarf; scared of water... Dragon Priests... boats... the dark... graveyards... and maybe a few other things.*

Lord Tostig- *drugged and captured with his men, by Rosencross; saved from slavery by Thiery and a dragon attack.*
Blagger- *one of Lord Tostig's warriors.*

Aramis- *captain of a band of mercenaries; McDougal's childhood torturer.*
Rush- *one of Aramis' mercenaries; proud, vain, hates Fergus Leatherhead.*

Lord McDougal- *paragon of chivalry, awkward hero, landless lord.*

Fergus Leatherhead- *faithful shield-bearer to Lord McDougal, ranger.*

Igi Forkbeard- *ex-slaver of Count Rosencross, joined McDougal's party.*

Mercy- *niece of the King, rescued from the Priests of Bachus.*

Gettlefinger- *aka Grimesby, aka Craven Dregs; head of Hradcanny's thespian society.*

King Strongbow- *warrior King, consumed with a drive to please the masses, unstable mind.*

Queen Miriam- *sad, lonely, and fearful that the king will slip into insanity.*

Princess Catrina- *seeker of self, pleasure, and the false gods.*

Witch Esla- *false prophetess seeking the demise of Lord McDougal.*

Squilby- *one of the masters of the Citadel, dwarf, delights in wickedness; runs the Death Hunt.*

Pip- *young sneak, quick, eager and loyal.*

Percival- *(Pup) 5 year old younger brother of Pip; beggar.*

Lunace, Ogre, and Goblin- *superstitious and greedy giants; captured Igi Forkbeard in book one.*

Horatio- *Thiery's white wolf, giant variety.*

Woolly- *Ubaldo's woolly mammoth.*

Birdie- *Oded's talking bird.*

Griz- *Oded's grizzly bear.*

Mamma- *matriarch of the badger clan, studied by Staffsmitten.*

Prologue

When last we met, the hunter's moon illuminating the night—the terrible night in which the beasts of the hunt spewed forth their crooning death song. Lord McDougal, faithful Fergus Leatherhead, gentle Mercy, and Igi Forkbeard turned their horses towards Hradcanny, and into the valley that lay between that great city and the cloistered fortifications of Bacchus and the Queen of Heaven. Bear with me as we bring the sun back into the evening sky, and relate a few more rudimentary chapters of the tale. Soon after, we will once again hear Hradcanny's central gate open its barred mouth—hyenae and Death-Hounds seeking a meal.

Correspondence

Diego Dandolo leaned towards the door, held his breath, and listened. An hour he'd been waiting *... why has the Chronicler not rung?*

There it was again. The faintest sound of scrolls unrolled and the gentle thud as scroll-weights were placed on the corners to hold them back. And yes, he was sure of it now, there was definitely a pigeon in there. Someone had sent another message and still the Chronicler had not confided in him.

Diego Dandolo pulled upon his black moustache, twirling his fingers as he did so, twisting until it hurt. A larger than average speck of dust caught his eye as it trespassed and came to rest upon his desk. He carefully pressed his finger on the offending particle when suddenly the silence was touched by the faint ringing of a bell.

Diego jumped from his seat and with three quick strides he stepped before his master's door, took a deep breath, and entered.

There was indeed a pigeon upon the window ledge, and it had been there a good while—two white blotches soiled the stone beneath it—Diego frowned. The Chronicler studied the writings before him without looking up, as if he had forgotten that he had rung for his assistant.

Diego approached a simple tapestry near the fireplace, pulled it aside exposing a narrow passage, and whistled. The bird flew from the ledge and disappeared into the passage beyond.

The Chronicler looked up at the sound. "My friend, come here that I may speak with you."

Diego Dandolo took a step towards the Chronicler, at an angle that brought him closer to the window and the sill he desperately wanted to clean. The Chronicler's bushy eyebrows spoke volumes; his left eyebrow sank low, while his right rose and blended with the hairline above. Diego deftly spun a few degrees on his leading heel and came directly to him.

"For too long, I have not played the man's part," the Chronicler began. "I've sought the knowledge and truth of God, my pen has wrought much, but upon the hearts of my heritage there is little to nothing written." A tear built up on the brim of his eye before rolling over its edge, leaving a wet trail behind. He grasped a letter to his breast. The forbidden letter. Oh, how Diego wanted to know the contents, for what a sway it held over the Chronicler's heart.

The Chronicler was the wisest and most Godly man Diego knew, but he also knew that it would not do to protest the Chronicler's self-abasing words; he would only grow quiet and solemn. So he waited.

"This came from Oded a few days ago." The Chronicler held out a small shred of pigeon-parchment with a note scrawled upon it:

Thiery is ded
I think it was poison
dragin preests?
I faled him, Oded the Bear.

"I'm very sorry," Diego said, "But you did serve Thiery well, and he followed our God."

"No, I did not even care to meet my own great-great-great-great-great-great grandson. Yes, I sent others to watch and protect him, but I could have been a father to him. God commands us to show to the generations to come the praises of the LORD, and His strength, and His wonderful works that He hath done, that the generation to come might know them, even the children which should be born; who would arise and declare them to their children: that they might set their hope in God.

"I was busy gaining honors and the esteem of men, but I understood not. I am like the beasts that perish. What kind of man invests so little into his own children, and his children's children? It is a selfish man, and a foolish man who does not see afar off. My lineage is hundreds, perhaps thousands strong, and few if any serve the God of Noah. They and I have become estranged; I thought my work was of the greatest importance. Just think what those multiplied hundreds could be doing for our LORD if I had been faithful to them."

"You paint a bleak picture," Diego said, "yet His mercies are new every morning."

The Chronicler smiled. "You are a good friend Diego, a faithful friend. Indeed God is good. Look at this. Oded sent it but two days ago." He produced a second pigeon-parchment with further misspelled words:

> *God brawt me Thierys sister Suzie.*
> *I gardean her now, Oded the bare.*

"A sister?" Diego asked.

"It seems so. I had thought all were sacrificed; yet it appears one more yet lives. To her then we will give our attentions, to her I will teach the ways and the words of God. I will talk of them when we sit in our house, and when we walk by the way, and when we lie down, and when we rise up—if only God will place her in my hands."

"If Oded has her," Diego said, "then does it not only require that we send for her, or go and get her?"

"If only it could be as you say. We will certainly seek her out. It's in the Lord's hands. This arrived a few hours ago." The Chronicler handed him yet a third pigeon-parchment:

> *Dragin preests stole Suzie, think they*

are heding to Radcany.
Help from Lord Micdoogle.
Just got Ubaldo with me,
meeting Micdoogle at Sevin Talins.

The full weight of the words suddenly struck Diego. "The Death Hunt," he whispered. "We only have a few hours."

"Yes." The Chronicler scribbled some notes as he spoke. "Perhaps they will be safe inside the cloister's walls before the hunt begins, but if not," he paused. "We will try and lend a hand."

"It's treason for those within the city to lift a hand against the riders of the Death-Hounds."

"Treason," the Chronicler mused, "treason. If I were caught outside the walls tonight, my friend, would you aid me?"

Diego did not hesitate. "You know I would."

"Well, these are our friends, and they are seeking to save the heritage that God has given me. If it comes to it, then Strongbow can decide whether or not I have committed treason. Anyway, we will not leave the city ourselves, and those who will help are already outside the walls.

"Send runners with these messages. One to my ship, and the other to Staffsmitten; he studies a clan of giant-badgers between Knuckers Pool and Hradcanny high-way where it dips into the valley. Send Morgan, he knows the place, and he knows how to deliver the message so that Staffsmitten's work is not disturbed."

Diego Dandolo placed the missives in his pouch and sped towards the door. He slowed his pace under the lintel and called back to the Chronicler. "Don't forget the Hunt-fest tonight. The king is expecting you. I've set out your attire, and a carriage will pick us up in an hour. Count Rosencross will be there."

Pip

Diego watched as the runners walked along the alley. There were only two places Squilby's sneaks could be hiding—a deep alcove on the opposite side of the street or a sewer grate further down. He'd seen them use both before to watch this particular door. Diego leaned, eye pressed to the peephole as he surveyed the scene before him; he wanted to ensure the runners were not followed. Once they were in the street, the runners would lead a merry chase, but if anyone could keep up with them, it was the sneaks. The peep gave a view of the alley's entire length; if they tried to follow he would know, and he would act.

It was Diego's particular pleasure to best them at their own game, for Diego Dandolo was once a sneak himself. A full twenty-years-ago it had been, before a late growth spurt disqualified him. At the time it was a terrible blow, for he was being groomed as a Death-Hound rider, one of the greatest honors a sneak could aspire to. Then the Master of the Citadel, the Chronicler himself, took him into his personal service; his love for the man grew, and he learned of the one true God.

The runners were almost to the street and nothing else had moved. If it hadn't been a sunny day and within the exact hour that the sun shone upon this alley, the sneak would have gone undetected. The only clue was that for a few seconds a shadow fell across the door. If the shadow had been more fleeting, Diego would have dismissed it as a passing bird. Having looked into the sky from the Chronicler's chamber moments before, Diego knew there were no clouds whatsoever.

Opening the door and leaping into the alley, Diego quickly realized the stratagem that had almost bested him. A window four stories above lay open. A rope ran taut the length of the alley to a metal ring embedded high on the wall just above the view one had when looking through the peep. A boy was racing along the rope, hand over hand, approaching the end of the alley, and as Diego ran, the boy disappeared around the corner.

There were only a few sneaks who could move so quickly along a rope, and Diego had a good idea who it might be. Diego reached the corner of alley and street just as a scrawny youth dropped to the ground.

"Pip!" Diego Dandolo shouted.

The youth shot into the crowd. Just before disappearing he turned back to glimpse the one who'd yelled his name. For a second their eyes met and then Pip was gone.

Diego tried to pick him out amongst the carts and people. Nothing.

Diego spun on his heel to find Pip standing before him taut as a pulled bow string, ready to spring away at any moment, smiling. His eyes fidgeted between Diego and the direction of the runners.

"Pip, at your service, sir. I've an important errand, requesting leave to go, sir." The words tumbled forth at an incredible speed, making them almost indiscernible.

"And your errand?"

A pained expression twisted Pip's face.

"Oh never mind," Diego said, "I'm sure I already know."

Pip smiled his gratitude—his bow-like figure once again ready to spring.

"Okay, then, who was it that gave you this errand?"

Pip's unpleasant expression returned, his shoulders slumping. There was no way he could follow the runners now. Diego felt pity for the lad, for causing him to fail in his mission.

"I mean no disrespect, sir," Pip said. "I just don't know as if I'm at liberty to say."

"Perhaps I can enlighten you then. I understand that I have put you in a difficult place, Pip. You owe Master Squilby much. He is your teacher and deserves respect as such.

"But you did right in coming back when I called you. While Master Squilby is of higher Citadel rank than I, he is not of higher rank than the Chronicler. I am on an errand for him; and those runners are on an errand for him. The Chronicler did not want sneaks or anyone else following them, so whose orders should you obey?"

"The Chronicler, sir." Pip sighed. The youth's eyes and cheeks looked a bit sunken, and he was pale. The street sounds hummed along, but they were not loud enough to hide a growl from Pip's stomach.

"Hold out your hands, Pip."

He did so without hesitation or comprehension. They shook.

"Doesn't Master Squilby feed you?"

"Oh, yes, sir, he takes good care of us."

Diego Dandolo looked intently into Pip's eyes. The youth averted his gaze. "Tell me the truth of it, and don't mix your words."

"Well it's like this, sir. I done messed up this job, and so I'll not get my dinner. You see, it's my fault. That's all there is to it." Pip looked up into Diego's eyes, and Diego did his best to raise one eyebrow the way the Chronicler would. Pip looked away again. "Well I guess there's a little more to tell about it."

He hesitated a moment. "I'm sure there's no harm in tellin' you that I've a little brother, and we go halvsies on all we take in, only he's just five, so he's not able to take in much yet. But we're doing just fine. He's a brave kid, and I've squirreled away a piece of bread for him, so he'll not go without somethin' tonight. And that truly is all there is to say on the matter."

Pip's smile returned and he once again looked up at Diego Dandolo.

"Well, I'll tell you a little more myself then. I'm impressed by the way you set up your ropes, and how you managed the whole thing so quick. I'm more impressed however with the character I see in you. I know the Chronicler will be as well when I tell him. Don't veil the conscience that God has given you, Pip. Here's a copper for your ingenuity and another copper for me being the cause of your lost dinner. Send my regards to your little brother. You're free to go then."

Pip glanced around the street and tucked the coins away without seeming to do anything but straighten his shirt. "Thank you, sir, thank you!" The next instant he was lost in the crowd.

Staffsmitten

Lately, Staffsmitten had been thinking about death.

At the time of the flood countless souls, descendants of Adam and Eve had all turned their backs upon the Lord and reveled in wickedness. Eight souls were found righteous before Him. Only eight souls. The rest had died.

And there was Enoch. He had lived 365 years before he was translated, that he should not see death. Enoch had this testimony: that he walked with, and pleased, God.

The descendants of Noah seemed always ready to turn to the other gods, false gods, demons masquerading as gods; man was quick to pursue the imaginations of his own heart.

Yet here at least there were still many who served the one true God.

And here, under the protection of Strongbow, he was able to look into academics, sciences, and other pursuits that allowed him to explore the great design of God's creation—it was superbly fascinating.

For two months he had been away from his gate-keeping duties; he sighed with the realization that he must soon return. Of course, he had exciting studies to return to there also; he just hadn't expected that he would grow so close to the clan.

This was his favorite place to observe and write—upon a massive singular boulder set carefully in the center of a glen at the base of slight hill. Before him was one of the many entrances to the badger clan's den—a twisting maze of tunnels and snug rooms, escape passages, and storage chambers. Staffsmitten even had his own quite comfortable quarters within.

To his right there was the burial mound, which seemed almost sacred to the critters of the clan, for they never crossed its crest.

Just this morning Mamma badger had buried a young fox there. It had broken a leg days before. He thought it might recover from its long fall, but it was not to be. Soon after the sun began to rise, Mamma appeared, carrying the limp fox gently in her teeth. She led a procession of animals; seven giant-badgers, two wolverines, another fox, and three juvenile skunks. They solemnly circled Mamma at the burial mound.

She dug quietly and quickly, laid the fox kit in its grave, and covered it up. The animals stayed for a few moments, looked from one to the other, and then wandered into the forest—a most remarkable event. It brought a tear to Staffsmitten's eye.

Yes, the badgers, especially Mamma, were proving to be one of his favorite studies. God had programmed into the badger the ability, even the desire it seemed, to adopt foundling critters. And so, after being accepted into the clan himself, Staffsmitten had begun to introduce various or-phaned litters to Mamma; the latest were the skunks.

She was a dutiful mother and a fierce protector. In fact, pound for pound it seemed there might not be a stronger mammal than the badger or wolverine, at least none that he had yet found. Mamma, being of the giant variety, was close to two-hundred pounds.

Thwump. The sound jarred his pen, splotching the par-chment with ink. Staffsmitten drew a curved blade, and reached into his pouch for his new invention—skunk bombs. Then he saw the arrow protruding from a nearby tree with something wrapped about its shaft.

Night came on fast in the valley, and at first the hunter's moon would not reach the valley's depths. But already the eastern slope was brightly lit; it had been almost from the setting of the sun.

Mamma sniffed the arrow that lay on the ground. Two of the clan entered the burrows and a moment later, emerged. They lifted their noses to the air.

The tall man-thing had wandered off again. Many of her little ones were *different*, but he was the most unusual. At first she had even been afraid but now she accepted him as one of them.

This arrow with its new smells made her uneasy. She hadn't seen the man all day, and so, with the clan in tow, she marched through the forest following his scent.

Hunt-Fest

C ount Rosencross was next. One bell tolled its warning that the hunt was soon to begin.

Then he was standing before the king. He kneeled and lifted Strongbow's hand to his forehead—a sign of subservient loyalty. Rosencross had rehearsed the exercise often, placating his pride with the thought that all must do it, and one day all would do it for him. Still, it was difficult.

Strongbow was evidently enjoying himself. Pulling Rosencross to his feet, he gestured to his wife and daughter. "Queen Miriam. Princess Catrina."

The princess was beautiful.

The king then motioned towards the count. "And this is Count Rosencross of Bannockburn." Rosencross bowed and kissed each lady's outstretched hand in turn. Then he stood to his full height and prepared to receive their admiration, especially that of the princess.

But king, queen and daughter had turned to meet the next guest.

It did not faze him though. He admired her for her stately purpose, knowing that her excellent breeding explained her modest reserve. He knew that, of course, his stature and striking looks had taken her breath away.

Turning, his eyes were met by those of Diego Dandolo, standing aloof near the battlements. Was he mocking? Laughing? Challenging with his smile? It was hard to tell, and now the man was coming his way. There was nothing to be done but meet him head on. Though he knew he could squash the small man with his greater physical strength, there was something about him that made Rosencross wary.

Diego gave a slight bow, really just a nod of his head. "Good evening, Count. I hoped that you would be here. I so wanted to see how you would dress for the occasion."

"Did you say, 'how I would dress'?" Rosencross could not help but feel that they were somehow sparring, and that Diego Dondolo was adept at keeping the upper hand without seeming to do so.

Entirely unpredictable, Diego's words at one stroke might be disarming while his expression and manner would lean as if to strike. Then his speech might smack of assault and yet his face and body bespeak friendship, even admiration. Then just as quickly both his countenance and language would retreat, offending not at all.

"But, of course. You and I were born, not just to wear our clothes, but to present them to an admiring audience, yes?"

Count Rosencross glanced about to see if anyone was watching. What was this annoying man up to? He could not tell if he was making fun, or just noting something of which he himself enjoyed partaking. The man was obviously taken with himself, going to great lengths to keep every article of clothing clean and arranged. But if others were watching, holding back smirks of their own, well then—that would not do. At all costs the Count must be a man that people feared to take lightly.

"In fact," Diego continued, "I took a chance and wore some gloves of my own. And I'm gratified to see that you have once again worn yours. Though, it is a bit warm." He methodically pulled each finger free and then removed his gloves. "Don't you think, Count? Too warm for gloves this evening?"

The sun was lowering fast. Guests were starting to gather near the battlements, and someone called out "There are riders on horseback, outside the cloister's gates!"

The conversation forgotten, both men leaned against the stones and peered across the grasses of the plateau, across the intervening valley, and squinted to make out the small forms at the Bachus and Urania cloister.

Suddenly, an arm passed in front of the Count's view. Annoyed, he looked toward the person who dared to be so rude. It was the Chronicler. He was holding a spyglass before the Count, and perhaps he was—yes, he was certainly offering the instrument for his use. The rising anger quickly subsided, but still he did not like how these two were able to keep him off balance.

"Thank you." Taking the spyglass he scanned the ground, found the cloister, then the gate, and then the horses. There were three horses, but four persons upon them. To his astonishment, he saw that one of them was Igi Forkbeard. Startled, he lowered the glass and saw that Diego Dandolo was studying him.

Rosencross shrugged his shoulders and passed the spyglass to Diego.

The king's voice rang out, "Diego, bring that to me."

It didn't seem possible for Diego to move as quickly and as gracefully as he did. But seconds later he was upon the kings platform handing him the requested instrument.

"It is Lord McDougal," the king's voice boomed in surprise, "and my niece!"

The Queen's hand went to her mouth. The princess looked pale. A robed, bent form appeared from the shadows and climbed the king's platform. Rosencross heard someone whisper, "It is the witch, Esla."

Once again Esla cried forth her curse, "Before the birthing of the sun at year's end, McDougal and all that stand with him, shall die."

Unsure, expectant, tense; the gathered crowd jumped as a bell rang out.

Again, and again it rang; soon the city sounds were drowned in a clanging ambuscade of bells. In that moment of terrible expectancy, from the same dark corner where the witch had appeared, a dwarf rushed forward. The guests melted away from him as he flipped, rolled, and almost flew through the air, leaping his way to the top edge of the battlement where he abrubtly halted his wild rush, teetering two-hundred feet above the moat and serpents below.

At the very moment the bells quieted and the dwarf teetered, the population of Hradcanny noticed the riders outside the cloister gate. A collective gasp rent the air and the dwarf fell.

Rosencross had been almost close enough to grab him. In fact, as he reached for his leg, the dwarf seemed to move it further away.

Rosencross looked up into his face then, and the dwarf smiled wildly, winking his bulging eye. There was no scream.

The Count leaned over the stone wall and looked down to see if the dwarf might survive the fall into the moat. What he saw, upon a ledge far below, took his breath away.

Dark wings spread at least thirty-feet wide; a creature launched into the air, plucked the dwarf from his descent, and then soared above the city.

A moment later Hradcanny's central gate opened its iron barred mouth, and the beasts of the hunt spewed forth in waves of gnashing teeth—crooning their death song.

A Plan

Fergus Leatherhead could feel the pressure building. The horses had traveled all day. Running back the way they came was out of the question. With McDougal and Mercy on one horse, and the bulk of Igi on another—they would never make it. But what then? Igi Forkbeard feared the false gods, and was most likely uncertain of his new master; would he stay?

McDougal took a deep breath and smiled. "It's nights like these that put you in awe of your Creator. Look at it, my friends."

"Sir," Fergus tried to whisper so that no one else could hear, "shouldn't we be going? We're about to be hunted down and, well, perhaps you could encourage the troops, as it were."

"What can be more encouraging than knowing that God is? That He is real, that He loves us, that He has made us and all this." McDougal pointed into the sky as he wheeled his horse into the valley. "When I consider thy heavens, the work of thy fingers, the moon and the stars, which thou has ordained; what is man, that thou art mindful of him? O LORD our Lord, how excellent is thy name in all the earth!

"Come my friends, let's do the unexpected."

Igi Forkbeard found his voice now, "What is that, sir?"

"We'll ride directly towards them, and then, to be honest, I'm waiting on God. For if we continued on, up the other side of the valley and into their onslaught, that would likely get us killed. Then there's a retreat, but I don't think that will get us very far either. We can follow the valley up into the mountains or down towards the river, but by the time we reach the valley's bottom we'll have to decide which.

"So, Fergus, tell us what to expect from these beasts that hunt so well. Don't leave anything out, the knowledge might save us."

"Yes, sir. It's rather disturbing, sir."

"Go on, Fergus, disturb us then; it will only give God more glory if we survive."

"Yes, sir. Well, we'll be hunted by three elements. The first are the hyenae. They are matriarchal; the oldest female leads them. Packs can run from twenty to a hundred members, though I think Squilby runs about eighty during the hunt.

"They are of the giant variety, weighing about three hundred pounds, with a hunched back, short hind legs, and powerful jaws that can crush bones. In fact, they don't leave anything behind when they eat—not the horns, hooves, tough animal skins, nor even bones. As a result, their excrement is chalk-white. The one thing they cannot digest is hair; they cough up large hair balls.

"They do not attack and kill as many animals do. They continue to chase, running their quarry down to exhaustion, taking bites, chunks of flesh at a time—ruthless really.

"But the characteristic I dislike most about the creatures is their maniacal laugh; most notable when in the presence of food. If we hear them cackling nearby then it will not be long before they attack us."

"Splendid description, Fergus, and the other two elements?"

"Well, there are many food sources the hyenae might pursue and therefore miss us altogether, except that Master Squilby is carried about by some giant winged creature. He likes to keep a mystery about it. Some say it is a bat of monstrous proportions, and others say it is a trained winged-serpent—a dragon. In any event, he directs the hyenae with whistles from the air and an imitation of their laughter. They can hear it and respond from at least two miles away.

"I've only met Squilby once, and something doesn't seem quite right about the man. I'm not sure, but I think he takes pleasure in seeing death around him. He's unsettling. I'm sure that he is our greatest danger, for if he knows we're out here, he'll most likely direct them towards us.

"Aiding him on the ground are his Death-Hounds. They are much larger than the hyenae, but what makes them especially dangerous are the men who ride them. Hand picked for their small stature, they are pure muscle trained in acrobatics, throwing weapons, and a difficult to master three-section staff. If we take to the trees to avoid the hyenae, these men will flush us out—"

"Listen!" McDougal held up a hand up for silence. They heard it then; hounds baying, and something else too. High pitched but muffled, it was the call of the hyenae. "They come."

"Halloo, the road." A voice called to them from the forest.

"Approach the road." McDougal called back. He held his bow half pulled, one arrow nocked, and two more dangling from his fingers. Fergus took up a position slightly forward, blocking anything that might hit Mercy. He noted that Igi calmly turned his horse sideways, and kept an eye on their rear; he would do nicely then.

All brought their weapons to bear.

A lean figure stepped from the trees, dressed in leathers, knee-high boots, a wide brimmed hat, and a long coat that swung open below his belt as he moved. On one side of his belt hung a short, curved sword, and on the other a large purse. Strapped tightly to his leg was a contraption that looked like a small crossbow. "Chronicler sent me. Be quick now. We'll be taking some animal trails. Let your horses follow me."

McDougal hesitated.

36

"That's Staffsmitten," Mercy whispered. "I think we can trust him."

In single file they wound their way through thick woods and underbrush. McDougal rode point, followed by Fergus, with Igi bringing up the rear. Occasionally they came out into the open—small clearings strewn with tall grasses and rocks. The moon was not high enough to give much light where they traveled, but the eastern slope on their left was as bright as night can be.

Traveling in silence for twenty minutes, each sound from the forest, each far away baying of the hounds, each whistle carried by the wind, caused them to pause, straining their ears for the first cackling of the hyenae.

They stopped in a glen just big enough for their party. "This is where I must leave you my friends. The path gets wider as you get closer to the river. When the trees begin to thin, you'll suddenly come upon a large clearing where the path will fork. Take the left only if you've been spotted, for it winds its way through the moon-light for a time. The right is denser, a little longer, and it comes out at Knucker's pool.

"Stay away from the pool's edge; the path follows a se-ries of terraces where the water flows into the river. The Chronicler has arranged for his ship to be anchored just off the bank near Knucker's pool. It's usually a skeleton crew and they'll likely be quite nervous bringing a flat boat in close to ferry you and the horses to the ship. Take it slow and easy. The Death-Hounds will have already spread out in twos or threes, but ..."

The horses ears and heads came up, no one moved.

A black shape covered their glen from the sky, but only for a moment, and then it circled. They could no longer see it, but its wings made a heavy thrumping against the air—like when a sail first fills with wind—the tops of the trees whooshed violently away from the direction of the sound. Then it was quiet.

Fergus could barely make out that Mercy was shaking. No one spoke. Occasionally they could hear something in the trees, but it could have been anything. A continuous rustling filled the air as the wind moved through the leaves that brushed the sky.

Seconds dragged by. "You'd better get moving," Staffsmitten said quietly. "May God keep you."

Fergus couldn't shake the feeling that they were being watched.

"But what will become of you?" McDougal asked.

"I've got my badger burrow to retire to. No doubt they're aware the forest is alive with danger and they're concerned for me. I'd bring you along, but the clan wouldn't accept you right off. If I continued with you, and you needed to run, I'd only slow you down.

"But take this," reaching inside his coat, he brought forth an object too difficult to distinguish in the dark. "It's a ram's horn, blow on it three times if you're in danger and me and the badger clan will come running. There's a hole in it that a leather strip runs through. I'll just tie it to your saddlebags, so as you can reach it in a hurry."

"Thank you, my friend. How shall we know if you need help from us? For if you ever need anything at all, God willing, I'll be there."

"Like I said, I don't have far to go, and I'll be safe with the badgers. If I need you, I have another horn in their burrow. I dare say though, those hyenae aren't likely to try and dig us out. They've tried before and regretted it.

"The trail is before you there." He pointed and then ran into the trees towards the western slope.

Something stirred.

A blade, sharp, and painted black—so that no light could reflect upon it and give away the man who held it—waited in the dark.

McDougal and his party turned their horses onto the trail.

The blade hung like a leaf among the branches, still, poised, and keen.

The trail was narrow—horse, saddles, human legs, all brushed against the leaves. Undergrowth reached for the trail, and then parted as the riders passed.

The blade reached, curved up, passed by McDougal's leg, paused at his tendon, and then flicked towards the saddlebags. The ram's horn fell into a waiting hand. Blade and horn slowly retreated under the forest canopy as the rest of the horses moved along unaware.

The lone figure stepped into the clearing. He stood about four feet tall with one bulging eye, and a wicked grin. Sheathing his black dagger, he put his fingers to his lips and whistled. In a moment the clearing darkened, and he was plucked into the sky.

The dwarf waited, waited; wind whipped through his hair as they soared over the treetop, and then he began to laugh.

It was no human laugh. It was the call of the hyenae.

And there would be no horn by which to call for help.

Strongbow

"I can't see what's happening!" Strongbow's voice boomed. "Where did they all go? I want to know what is happening!" The veins in his neck and forehead protruded from under his skin, blue and pulsing.

The guests, startled, tried to act as if nothing out of the ordinary had occurred. But the memory of Strongbow's father, and his consuming madness, was likely amongst their thoughts.

As in a game of chess, pieces begin to move.

The queen retreats from the platform, her face drawn. Just before she disappears through a door, Rosencross sees her hand lift towards her eye as if she wipes a tear.

The witch Esla moves. Standing beside the king, her bent form straightens some, and her hood falls back slightly, revealing a smile, a young smile.

A Dragon Priest from amongst the guests looks over at Rosencross, who nods. The priest steps diagonally through a space between two knights and places himself to the side of the platform. His bald head and face are marbled with blue serpents, his eyes peer through the tattooed coils, and his mouth unites with that of the serpent etched on his face.

The Chronicler ascends the platform.

Two scribes write feverishly all that takes place.

"Ah ha!" Strongbow bellows and points a finger at the Chronicler. "Why has not Squilby flushed them from the valley? I can't see. Squilby knows that I want to see what is happening. You are Master of the Citadel, what do you have to say for him?"

"My King, as a great hunter yourself, you are aware that the hunted do not always purpose to go where the huntsman would like them to."

Not a sound could be heard, except the agitated breathing of the king. All knew that the Chronicler, one of the ancients from Babel, rarely spoke in public. All leaned forward to hear each word.

Strongbow's extended hand was shaking. He pulled it to his breast. There was a distant baying of a hound, and Strongbow's head cocked; his eyebrows raised; his mouth fell open.

The Chronicler drew him back by motioning to the crowd. "Men will watch for you, my King. If the hunt comes back into view, then they will let us know. Meanwhile your hunt-fest continues, and we've not heard from the bards yet. The night has proven most captivating to your subjects. Perhaps a song?"

It was then that Strongbow looked about. For a moment he seemed surprised to see the many faces surrounding him. "Of course, my subjects would like a song." He sat down upon his gilded chair. Princess Catrina laid her hand upon his arm.

There was a murmur of approval from the guests. The bard approached the platform.

"It will not be easy." Diego Dandolo spoke in hushed tones to Count Rosencross.

"What will not be easy?"

"To calm the king, to keep his mind from the hunt, to keep his mind ..."

Rosencross understood the unspoken words, but was surprised that Diego would dare to even hint at such things. Rosencross only strove to keep his eyes locked on those of Diego—he would not say a word, but he would not look away either.

"The Chronicler says," continued Diego, "the further a people, and the further kings, distance themselves from their God and therefore pursue the things of darkness, the further their minds become unstuck.

"The kings of the earth set themselves, and the rulers take counsel together, against the LORD, and against his anointed, saying, 'Let us break their bands asunder and cast away their cords from us.'

"He that sits in the heavens shall laugh. Be wise therefore, O ye kings: be instructed, ye judges of the earth. Serve the LORD with fear, and rejoice with trembling. Oh that they were wise, that they understood this, that they would consider their latter end! Those that turn away, their minds become unstuck from truth, from what is right. Unstuck."

Rosencross wrenched his eyes away, and instead stared at the spot where the bard was now beginning to sing. He could feel Diego's presence at his side, and was sure that the annoying man was looking at him.

It was a new ballad, and sung with a beautiful and emotive voice. Men clenched fists and teeth; women clung tight to whatever was near. The bard held his audience.

Rosencross could feel his face hot with anger, and then the blood drained away till he felt white and still, as if he himself stood on the precipice of death.

The bard sang on:

Baldwin's wife, again she called, come home,
To right, to love.

The priests of Baal they called,
Their voices were like the gods,
Bring us incense in the valleys, on the hills,
In the high places, and under every green tree,
That we may lift you up,
That we may lift you up.

Lords Belfry, Clovis, Baldwin, and Arsuf,

Ready were they with incense, with incense to lift them up.
Baldwin's sword cleaved the head of Clovis,
And Belfry, Baldwin, and Arsuf were lifted up.
Aye, they were lifted up.

Baldwin's wife, a tear,
A call to home,
To right, to love.

The giant's rear, the Priests inflamed,
The god's voices calling, an image of wood, of silver, of gold.
The enemies are coming, six fingers on their hands,
Yet an image of wood, of silver, of gold,
That we may lift you up,
That we may lift you up,

Lords Belfry, Baldwin, and Arsuf,
Ready were they with idols, with idols to lift them up.
Baldwin's sword, in twain made Belfry,
And Baldwin and Arsuf were lifted up.
Baldwin and Arsuf were lifted up.

Baldwin's wife, three children now,
A call to home,
To right, to love.

Man's own glory is what he wants,

PALADINS

The gods are calling blood, your children must,
Your children must be sacrificed to blood.
That we may lift you up,
That we may lift you up.

Lord Baldwin severs life from one, that he'll be lifted up.
Arsuf grows, and Baldwin then, he severs number two.
That he'll be lifted up. That he'll be lifted up.

Baldwin's wife, one child now,
A faint cry, a fevered brow,
A call to home,
To right, to love.

Still Arsuf grows, his kin to lean on Baldwin's land,
Yet still the gods do call,
'Baldwin, Baldwin, your child, to lift you up.'
That we may lift you up.

So Baldwin, gives a sacrifice, a sacrifice on high,
His child, his child,
His child to lift him up.

Baldwin's wife, no child now,
The arm of Arsuf is lifted up,
Baldwin's wife, a fever,
A whisper ... home ... right ....

Baldwin's wife asleep, to sleep,
And cry no more.
Baldwin's wife, she cries no more.

Rosencross felt the tears, he couldn't tell if they were apparent to others yet, but he was sure they were coming. Diego seemed a shadow on his right; the platform was before him, and somewhere to his left, the stairs.

He moved.

Somehow the stairs were before him, winding down to the street. His eyes stung and blurred, but each foot found a step, down and down he went.

He stumbled into the street. It was dark, and the moon did not reach where he walked, yet still he moved, until an alley showed darker than the brick on either side. Rosencross knelt into that dark, curled in on himself, and cried, and shook, and cried.

Diego Dandolo turned away, and he too allowed a tear to streak his face.

Hyenae

Human, inhuman, it was hard to tell. But those who heard that sound felt the fear of it, and many there were who said it had the timbre of evil in its notes. Worse yet, this laughter of the hunt seemed to come from the tops of the trees.

"Did you hear that?" Igi Forkbeard forced the whispered words through clenched teeth. "We've offended the gods, and now they've come for us!"

Fergus could feel his horse quiver. Birdie nuzzled her head under his chin.

Mercy tensed, and clutched McDougal's back.

McDougal jerked on his reigns, pulling up just before the clearing that Staffsmitten had spoken of, his hand raised for silence.

In the distance, they heard the answering call, excited laughter; much of it.

"Squilby knows where we are, sir," Fergus said. "And he's calling the rest to us."

"Oh LORD," McDougal called out, "where is Oded? Please send him to our aid. To your glory we ride, into your keeping we commend our souls." He squeezed his mount with his legs, drawing bow and arrow as they slowly stepped into the clearing, letting his horse have its head.

The high-pitched cackling was getting close.

"They move fast, Fergus, choose our path."

"It's been chosen for us, sir, look there!"

There at the rocky side of the clearing to the east, the trail that wound along the cliffs and Knucker's Pool was blocked.

A Death-Hound and rider barred the way, silent. The hound's lips curled back.

Their horses were tired but willing to push on. Sensing danger, all three sped towards the western path. Its entrance was wide and illuminated by the rising moon.

Fergus watched the Death-Hound, but it did not come. Its small rider stood upon the saddle and withdrew something from his vest. He then flung his arm with tremendous rapidity. Three shiny objects flew through the air towards them, arcing high; they would fall very near the path they were approaching.

The first dart fell just shy of them.

Fergus kicked at his horse's flanks, spurring him forward. He prayed.

The second dart flew high of its mark.

The third would come dangerously close to hitting McDougal or Mercy.

Reaching forward with his hickory spear, Fergus leaned over his horse's head. The thundering hooves, imperfect light, and small size of the dart in motion, made for an improbable feat, but he could think of nothing else.

The dart shot in toward the fleeing target of horse, man, and lady. Fergus reached, almost falling from his mount, and then he fell back into his saddle again. He glanced at McDougal, and then at the end of his hickory spear.

A three-inch dart was stuck in its end.

The clearing now behind them, they clung to the trail, slowing for the curving, undulating land, and the branches which might swipe a rider from his seat.

Those who would survive this night, in nights to come, would often wake trembling with sweat, from a dream—a nightmare in which they would hear again the tittering cackle; a sinister clamor of beasts, coming closer and closer.

The hellish chorus was chaotic as it filled the air, drowning horse hooves and hammering hearts. Snatches of black and brown mottled fur ran among the trees.

The horses were slowing even more still, too exhausted to outrun the cackling beasts.

Hyenae teeth showed against black muzzles in the moonlight. Their sneering visages coupled with eerie laughter, seemed like so many wicked smiles dancing in the dark.

Suddenly a hyenae's jaw opened at Fergus's leg. He slammed the butt of his spear into the side of its head, and then another leapt at him from higher ground. Fergus ducked and the beast tumbled past, almost knocking him from his saddle.

McDougal was stabbing to either side with his sword, and Fergus could hear Igi's battle cry just behind him.

They rode on, slashing, stabbing, then given a moment of respite, only to be attacked again. Still they rode, and then finally, a few hundred yards before them, they could see light shining upon water. The black river.

Just as suddenly, the din had fallen behind them. Though it seemed more frantic and alarming, at least it was not at their heels. Fergus and McDougal turned in their saddles at the same moment.

Igi's horse was twenty or so strides behind them, blood streaked flanks, heaving sides, and white froth at its lips. But its saddle was empty.

Igi Forkbeard was gone.

"Switch mounts with me, Fergus."

Fergus leapt from his saddle instantly. He dared not contradict McDougal in the midst of battle or strife, when a moment's hesitation could ruin his master's plans. But how he wanted to argue now. He knew that McDougal was going back to get Igi, and he knew that he must take Mercy to safety.

"Stay with her, Fergus," McDougal said, calm but stern, as he gathered the reigns of Igi's horse. "Once she's on the ship do not come back for me. If anything should happen, Mercy must have a protector. And you are my man." It was not a question. Fergus would do his duty.

McDougal smiled his boyish grin. "I'll be but a moment, and I'd very much like a cup of tea upon my return—if you don't mind."

"Eat him up, you pretty things." Squilby smiled, rubbing his hands together. He turned to the great winged beast perched on the limb next to him. "Isn't it beautiful, my princess?"

Igi Forkbeard had his back to a boulder. That was a pity, it might take longer to bring him down. And there were still the others to hunt. Squilby knew he should go and trail them, but he wanted to see this man's final battle. He knew the king would want to know of it.

At least four of the hyenae had died along the trail, and many of the others had stopped to eat their fellows. Still, there were about thirty here, and no lone man was going to kill thirty hyenae.

There was blood on Igi's arms and legs—whether his or theirs it was difficult to tell. He rested the tip of his great two-handed sword upon the earth. His chest heaved, and his head slumped.

The hyenae burst from the trees. Igi's head came up and his sword cut large swathes through the air, checking the charge.

One came too close. Its head cleaved, the beast dropped.

Again the hyenae retreated to the forest with frantic howling, whining laughter.

"He no longer shouts his battle cry when you come, my pretties," Squilby spoke soothingly to the night air. "He tires methinks. You'll get him on the next, but hurry, there's more food to be had."

Igi grabbed the dead hyenae by its back legs and swung him once in a circle—all three-hundred pounds—and then tossed its corpse into the yapping wood. More excited chaos ensued as they pounced upon the kill.

Legs buckling from the exertion, Igi dropped to one knee, and reached for his weapon. The lower ranking of the pack, which would not be allowed a morsel of the dead hyenea, came warily towards Igi once again.

"How he must thirst," Squilby mused. "No doubt his canteen is with his horse. I wonder if it was wise to throw such a heavy animal. It gave him some time, but was the exertion worth it? For I can see now that the bloodstains spread on his leg. Ha, then—it is his blood, and it flows, and he weakens, and he will die. But let's see, perhaps he'll cull the pack of one or two more. Make it good, Igi Forkbeard, and you shall have one more song sung at the hearth-fires."

They rushed in, sensing his fatigue. Igi swung again, and again, but still they came. His sword bit true, but he could not keep them at bay any longer; he was enveloped in a snarling mass.

Yet, It was he who snarled and fought the fiercest.

This time, when they retreated to the wood, many bled, and three lay dead about the man. Igi dropped to both knees now, using his sword as a staff to keep himself erect. His body, punctured and scratched.

He raised his face to the sky.

"Oh no, that won't help." Squilby chuckled. "The gods will not take you from me now. Make your peace, Igi. I salute you, that was a splendid show. I would almost intervene in honor of that fight, but I think it makes a better story to see it through to the end."

Igi's head fell forward.

His right hand slipped from the sword, limp.

He tottered.

Then two strong arms were lifting him to his feet, helping him into a saddle. Lord McDougal said something that Squilby couldn't hear. Then McDougal and Igi Forkbeard rode out at a trot.

The remaining hyenae attacked, but not the escaping men; it was the easy meal of their dead fellows that they engaged.

"Now that adds spice to the tale." Squilby fingered the ram's horn hung about his neck and petted his winged beast. "But I think we'll pen a different end than the one that they're expecting. Come, my princess."

A Cup of Tea

The ship lay anchored two-hundred or so feet from the bank. She was a four-mast galleon capable of extended trips out to sea, one-hundred-and-seventy feet long and forty feet wide in the beam. Her top castles extended far into the moonlight, and a man with bow or crossbow stood in each.

A rowboat waited only twenty feet out into the river, and quickly drew up as Mercy and Fergus came along the path. There were two rowers and two men armed with pikes. They refused to lay down their weapons and help Fergus with his horse. Their heads darted back and forth as they watched the woods, and they cringed at the sounds of the Death Hunt. One of the pike-men called out, "Leave the animal to fend for itself."

"I thank you for coming to our aid, but unless you've been ordered to leave the horse behind, I'll bring him with all the same."

The man seemed to waiver.

Fergus gave the horse a great shove, while Mercy jumped on board and coaxed the reigns.

If it had not been for the horse's exhaustion, Fergus could not likely have forced him onto the small craft; as it was, he gave in to their efforts. There was not much room now to move about, and the boat rolled a bit unsteadily, but the sailors at the oars pulled hard, and the boat made its way.

"Will he make it back to us?" Mercy asked, as she laid her hand and head upon the horse's neck.

Fergus stood on the other side of the large stallion; he couldn't see Mercy's face. "He has always come through before."

"But now, do you think he will now?"

"I hope, and I pray, and I will accept God's will to be done. But with a man's eyes and understanding I do not see how he can."

"Oh."

"But, if there were any man who could, I would say that Lord McDougal is that man. And Oded is out there somewhere, do not forget him."

"That is nice to think of," Mercy said, "and with God all things are possible."

"Yes, with God, all things are possible."

Fergus realized then that Birdie was no longer on his shoulder, and he wondered if the bird would find him on the morrow, or if it had been hurt or even killed during the chase. Death was all around and his heart felt heavy; but he had done his duty, and he would continue to do so. Fergus would keep the charge that McDougal had given him.

The boat bumped against the ship's side. Faces appeared at the rail, and a rope ladder swung over. Mercy climbed nimbly to the top.

Fergus glanced back toward the woods, fearful that McDougal would make it to the river, against all odds, only to be beaten down because there would be no boat to carry him in. Maybe he should have left the horse behind.

A sling, borne by block and tackle was lowered. The two sailors rigged it under the horse's belly. An instant later, it was carried up and onto the deck where water and oats were waiting. Fergus fairly flew up the ladder.

"Fergus Leatherhead," a familiar voice said, accompanied by a strong hand reaching towards him, "it warms my heart to see you again."

It only took a moment, and then Fergus smiled, grasping the hand and shaking it heartily. "Lord Tostig, it's very good of you to say so, sir."

"Where's McDougal?"

"One of us fell from the saddle as we rode. When we became aware of it, Lord McDougal commanded me to bring the lady to safety and assume the office of her protector until his return. He rode back for the other man."

"I've always liked him." Tostig leaned over the ship's side and called to the boat below. "Back to your post, Lord McDougal is still expected."

The boat pushed off and made its way toward the shore.

"And you, sir, why are you here, on this ship, of all places?" Fergus asked.

"Duplicity!"

Fergus raised his eyebrows.

"Yes, I don't know the half of it. But, my men and I were drugged and on our way to be sold as slaves. The man-stealer who raised his hand against us goes by the name of Count Rosencross."

Fergus raised his brows yet higher still.

"So you've heard of him then. Well, the Chronicler seems to think there's more to it than just slaving, otherwise I'd find this Count Rosencross and deal him his justice. But Lords Hasting, Utrecht, and Felton have not come in for the games. And what do they have in common with myself? We all serve the God of Noah, and not just with our lips, but with our whole heart, mind, and soul.

"So, he's asked me to stay hidden, and his ship is where he's put me. I'm not sure there's another man I'd do such bidding for, but at least this night has given us some adventure." He turned to Mercy then, "I've had my things moved from my cabin, so that you may have some privacy. My Lady, please take no offense, but you look done in. Would you like to rest now?"

"Thank you, Lord Tostig," Mercy replied. "But I cannot go, not until I see what has happened. Perhaps though, someone could bring a cup of tea."

"Forgive me, lady, it will be done directly."

Tea in hand, Mercy stared hard, blinking sleep away. The ship creaked and gently swayed. Fergus saw her head lean slowly aft, then snap back to wakefulness.

Out from the teacup, a few drops splashed on her hand. She'd not had even a sip of it.

Again the terrible laughter echoed throughout the wood.

There was a whistle from the mizzen's top-castle, and then all the crew grew attentive to shadows moving along the bank. "Is it them?" Mercy whispered.

"I believe it is." Fergus grinned. "See how the rowboat approaches the bank. They'd not do that if it were an enemy."

The boat and shadows disappeared, swallowed by the dark of an inlet, choked by thick branches that reached over the water as if to grasp with gnarled fingers.

"Oh, but they are gone long," Mercy sighed, "It is so dark in there." She shuddered as if in remembrance of that valley of death; the snarling teeth, the air borne beast, and the sounds. Collectively they could still one's heart with tingling dread that trickled down nerves and spine.

Seconds passed into minutes.

The bow birthed from the dark; amidships then, the rowers pulled into the moon streaked waters. Pike-men held the stern, last to shed the grasp of vine and branch that clenched and then let go.

"No one," Mercy gasped. "Fergus, there is no one else upon that boat."

Out from the teacup, another splash, bigger than the first, wet the deck.

But as the boat lay alongside the Chronicler's ship, a tall form could be seen prostrate along the keel.

Lord Tostig enquired of his men whether or not it was McDougal. The same rig that carried the horse was lowered towards them.

"It's not sir, he wouldn't come, said there wasn't enough room for the horses and his wounded man. We tried to convince him not to stay, but we'll be back for him in a jiffy."

It took all four of the men to lift and strap the unconscious Igi Forkbeard to the sling. Up and over the rail he came, guided down easy by the hands of Fergus and a couple of Tostig's men. He was bruised, bloodied, and begrimed. So much so, that one could not make out who he was.

The rowboat pushed off.

No bed was large enough on board to lay his body on, and fearing to move him more they lay Igi upon the deck; a lantern was brought near to work by. Mercy called for boiled water, clean linens, and any doctor's kit that may be on hand. She set the cup of tea just inside a scupper where it was not likely to be harmed.

Halfway there, the rowboat plied on.

With eyes rimmed red, Mercy cleaned and sewed shut the worst of the wounds. "It is not that any one is so bad, but that there are so many, and so much loss of blood," She said out loud to no one in particular.

Swallowed hole, the rowboat found the bank.

Seconds passed again to minutes.

Mercy tended her patient.

Suddenly, the air was rent by a new sound. One blast—a second blast—then the third blast of a distant horn.

Fergus glanced at Mercy and her eyes bore into his, questioning, fearful. He answered her look with the words, "It is why I love him so."

The boat arrived; it held upon it two horses quite near death, two rowers, two pike-men, and a message carried by the last. "Lord McDougal says that he regrets his being detained further, but Master Staffsmitten has called for help and he feels himself obliged to answer the call. He says not to worry if he does not return this evening, for the tree tops might be safer than making a return trip, at least until the morning comes."

Again, three horn blasts beckoned.

An unfortunate placement of a sailor's foot knocked Mercy's cup of tea, through the scupper, its contents spilled; it vanished with a splash.

Ambush

"**M**uch better, my princess," Squilby whispered. "Yes, a much better ending than I dared hoped for."

The winged terror and Squilby, perched once again high in the trees, overlooked the large clearing where the three paths converged. One from Hradcanny high-way, one from Knucker's Pool, and the last—the longer route to the river, where the hyenae still cackled over their feast.

The moon made clear every tuft of grass. But the forest was in places black, in others darkened grey—like a wall of shadows, encircling, standing watch over the glade.

Squilby put the ram's horn to his lips and blew three more times. He chuckled.

"Oh, the waiting. I can't bear it. Let us, you and I, my pretty, philosophize together to pass the time.

"My students tell me that the Chronicler said the most untenable thing. Tell me what you think of it, don't be shy, I'm sure we'll be agreeing, you and I. So here's his speech, 'They that feared the LORD spoke often one to another: and the LORD hearkened, and heard it, and a book of remembrance was written before him for them that feared the LORD, and that thought upon his name.'

"But I say, what good is a mere mentioning in a book that no one will read. And why fear God whom we do not see. The gods that you and I serve, now they shall profit a man with power and glory. The God of Noah, he it is we mock, oh but it is vain to serve God: and what profit is it to those who keep his ways.

"I see you are disgusted by the Chronicler as much or more than I. I knew you would see it aright. Let me stir your gut some more; listen further to his chatter. He says, 'Then shall ye return, and discern between the righteous and the wicked, between him that serveth God and him that serveth him not. For, behold, the day cometh, that shall burn as an oven; and all the proud, yea, and all that do wickedly, shall be stubble: and the day that cometh shall burn them up, saith the LORD of hosts.'

"Admittedly those are fine and high sounding words. But it is folly just the same. Here is truth for you my princess. We call the proud happy and those that work wickedness are set up; yes, they that tempt God are even delivered. You can see as well as I what is occurring all around us, it is even what we are about this night.

"Those that serve the God of Noah would bind us with rules, laws, and ordinances that hinder a man beyond what should be. I say, let us break their bands asunder, and cast away their cords from us. I see you tremble with the mean-

ing of my words. A right good companion you are my
pretty."

Squilby put his finger to the side of his protruding eye,
and pushed. It bulged further; increasing and decreasing the
pressure, he changed its shape by degrees, bringing distant
details into focus; he scanned the edges of the clearing,
looking for signs of arrival.

He was about to blow the horn again when a movement
caught his eye. Moon-glint on a curved sword that was
inching from the path, the one that led back towards the
high-way. It was Staffsmitten, and then a bit of a surprise—following him, were a number of ambling skunk,
wolverine and giant badgers.

Squilby's eyes narrowed. He had to admit that the odds
were worse now. It was one thing to lose some hyenae, but
the Death-Hounds and their riders were too valuable to lose
in a melee in which the outcome might be less certain. And
while the hyenae were engaged, he did not want to squander
the advantage of surprise by waiting for another opportunity.

He knew what to do.

First, he must keep them where they were until
McDougal came to answer the summons of the ram's horn.
See what fools these men of God, men of honor, were!
Their high ideals would bring them both out of hiding, and
into certain destruction.

Soon the winged beast was circling high above the trees, sometimes swooping over the clearing, sometimes just out of sight, but always the loud thrumming of its wings told of its proximity.

Staffsmitten and the badger clan melted back into the edge of the forest.

After five minutes, the flying beast came to perch, and Squilby leaned forward to watch, pushing upon the swelling bulge that was his eye.

Five minutes more and Staffsmitten, tentatively breached the wood. He took two steps into the clearing. There was an answering step from McDougal's long legs, across the way, at the entrance of the path from Knucker's Pool.

They closed the gap, swift, silent.

The badger clan hung back a little, uncertain of the stranger.

So then, the trap was sprung.

With wicked glee, Squilby screeched the perfect call of an owl. He screeched again.

Sudden cracking of twigs, rustling of leaves, from all directions, and the shadows that circled the clearing were filled with new shapes. The forest came alive with Death-Hounds eager to close in.

But close in they did not. Each rider, with vest open, looked to be rapidly beating their chests and waving their arms. Each hand deftly picked dart or knife from vest scabbards and whirled them in the air, over and over. From where Squilby sat, the moon reflected and blurred on those tiny dots of steel.

He thought it almost pretty.

A Terrible Blow

"Wake up children, wake up!" Gimcrack fairly shook from head to foot. "Oh, the witch was right. It's all so terrible!"

Thiery and Suzie woke with a start. Horatio leapt to his feet, and stood at the top of the winding stairs, peering into the gloomy depths from which Gimcrack had just emerged.

"I'd have let you sleep the day away, but this news cannot wait, or I'll most certainly burst my brain, and then where will you poor children be? Do you know, all this agitation cannot but surely bring on some kind of apoplexy? In fact, I'm sure if things continue the way they've been going, it's likely I'll be dead by the end of the week!"

"Oh dear!" Suzie started, covering her mouth.

"Yes, do you know," continued Gimcrack, encouraged by Suzie's exclamation, "that I once had an uncle who looked very much the way I feel. He complained of this ache, and this stress, of chilblains and of general malaise. And then, when he was partaking of his evening pipe—to calm the nerves as he would say—he just up and died. Just like that. Dreadful, is what it is."

"You look healthy to me," Thiery said, hoping to encourage his friend.

"That's exactly my point. My uncle looked perfect health itself."

"But you just said that you feel as bad as he looked."

"Yes," Gimcrack looked befuddled. "It wasn't so much his constitution I was addressing, but his facial expressions which told the true story of it. Oh, I'm afraid your young minds can't grasp death and disease in the way that I do. I can't expect you to appreciate my poor condition. But we delay—on to my news! Prepare yourselves, for it is terrible indeed. Just one more nail in my coffin, as it were.

"It turns out that the riders we saw last night were none other than Lord McDougal's party. That great and bold man, with only two others, rode into the midst of a Bachus priest sacrifice, and stole the sacrifice from under their noses. What's more amazing is that it was the king's niece."

"Hooray for Lord McDougal," Suzie cried out with flushed face and clapping hands.

"Yes, and one of the two riders with him was Fergus Leatherhead—which of course makes perfect sense—but the second was none other than Igi Forkbeard. How is that for amazing?"

Thiery was surprised, for Igi had seemed quite vexed when last they met. Yet then again, at times he seemed to really want to know who the God of Noah was; and the three of them had been praying for the man. He smiled to think of Igi riding with Lord McDougal; perhaps he would leave the selling of human lives behind him, and perhaps McDougal would convince him of the one true God.

"Did they get away?" Suzie asked.

"For all the talk in the streets, it seems they did, and they didn't."

"Oh, no."

"Yes, little one. Alas it is the way of the world. The Lady Mercy, Fergus, and Igi seem to have disappeared. Some say they'll not find anything of them either, for nothing is ever left of a hyenae's meal. Still others say that they got away, and are in hiding or healing. You see, eighty-two hyenae and ten Death-Hounds went on the hunt. All the hounds returned, but only sixty five hyenae came back. It is a thing to be sung about."

"And Lord McDougal," Thiery asked, "what has become of him?"

"That is what I hesitate to tell." Gimcrack glanced at Suzie with a most troubled look. She buried her head in her blanket for fear of the news. "Yes, little one, it is bad. The Death-Hound riders brought in two men. I don't know how Staffsmitten came to be one of them. I had prepared myself for the probability of his death when he was nowhere to be found, though I don't know how he came to be out last night amongst the hunt, but there it is. Our little cave won't be the same without him.

"The second man was Lord McDougal; I'm very sorry for it. It's a terribly sad business. Our faithful friend is dead."

"Oh, no, that can't be!" Suzie grabbed Gimcrack's rough hands. "Please don't say that."

Gimcrack's eyes shifted softly and he swallowed with obvious effort.

Suzie's tears were falling now. "Please, Gimcrack sir, please say he's safe."

"I ... um ... he's ..." but Gimcrack didn't need to say anything more, for his sad, pitying face told the truth more than words could.

Suzie fell upon her pillow.

Thiery patted her back as she cried and Horatio licked the side of her face as both he and Gimcrack sat beside her, hoping their close proximity would somehow bring some comfort.

After a while she lifted herself up upon her pallet and spoke, an occasional and involuntary intake of breath intruding upon her discourse. "I remember what he said. I think it when I go to sleep. He said he was my true friend, and the guardian and watcher for my soul. Isn't that a beautiful thing to say?

"But, in my mind, I made him more than that." Suddenly she looked sheepish. "Oh, but I guess it was silly of me."

"No, he was a grand man." Gimcrack smiled. "I didn't know him long either, and I feel his death almost as keenly as Staffsmitten's, who I've known for years. Come, now, tell us what he was to you, child."

"Well, he seemed like he would be a very good Daddy." More tears rolled down her cheeks

"Suzie," Thiery said with great tenderness, "I'm sure he would have thought you were the best of daughters—you're a treasure."

"Thank you Thiery, that's a beautiful thing to say too. Thank you for saying it. I'm sure it will be very nice to think about when I go to sleep. God is so very good to give me a brother like you." Suddenly she smiled through her tears. "You know, I thought you were dead once, and God brought you back to me again." She looked into their eyes, hopeful.

Thiery and Gimcrack smiled back at her, a sad sort of smile.

Suzie, perceiving their look, clasped her hands together; her big eyes looked bigger still. "He might, and it doesn't hurt to ask. God loves me."

"As long as you know," Thiery said, "that he still loves you even when he doesn't give you the things asked for."

"Yes, I do."

"And think," Thiery continued, wanting to make his point perfectly clear, "of all the children, and the wives, and the husbands, who must have asked for such a thing of God. I don't say that He can't or won't do it, only that He obviously doesn't do it very often. He has his reasons—according to the purpose of Him who works all things after the counsel of His own will—so please don't put too much hope in the answer you would like to hear. Keep your hope and faith in God Himself, no matter what He sees fit to do, that we should be to the praise of His glory."

"Yes, I will." She sniffled, and then hugged her brother.

Gimcrack served them bread and cheese for lunch which he had brought from his morning excursion through the city. Then he set before them the situation as he saw it. It was generally agreed upon that the Dragon Priests and Count Rosencross must be avoided; they could fairly assume that Thiery, Suzie, and Gimcrack would forfeit their lives if they once again came under their power.

While agreeing that it was important to find Oded, they had no idea where to look. Fergus might be of assistance to them, but again they did not know where to find him, or even if he lived. They could not expect much from the Dwarven Brotherhood either, as they had entrenched themselves in Tump Barrows—with ominous events spreading through their ranks like a canker.

The trio had little in the way of provisions, and no good means for cooking, for the Dwarven Brotherhood kept their way-stations comfortable but sparse. Somewhere in his travels Thiery's pouch had come undone; lost to them was the small pile of coins from Igi Forkbeard's men. Gimcrack had four coppers. Thiery still had two gold pieces, and four silvers sewn into his clothing.

"A month I'm thinking," Gimcrack surmised, "and then our funds will be used up."

"We need employment then," Thiery said. "I can surely find something."

"Yes, we will certainly try. It is only that when I'm engaged as a mapmaker, it is usually to be sent on some expedition. That would take me away from you both, this I would rather not do. Perhaps I could find something at the Citadel. Many of the scribes find the copying of maps a tedious business.

"And there are some positions for promising young men there. The difficulty lies in getting a recommendation. The Citadel is an unusual and splendid place, but a boy cannot just walk in the front gate and apply. And while I have access to the library and scribes because of my occupation, I would be severely reprimanded or possibly even lose my privileges if I were to bring you in.

"There is one way though. I hesitate to mention it, for it has its hazards."

"Please tell me," Thiery said. "I'm eager to help."

"Well, with the fair about to begin, it could be excellent timing to make yourself known. Every year at the festivities, men and boys lose their lives or at least their livelihood due to injuries sustained. The masters of the various depart-ments end up with vacancies.

"There is one master in particular who allows unan-nounced inquiries. He specializes in working with foundling or street boys, but he is a dangerous man; the Dwarven Brotherhood has expelled him from their midst. He is none other than Master Squilby, the leader of the Death Hunt."

"Oh, I see." Thiery sat quietly for a while before speak-ing. "Would it be wise to purposefully place myself under his authority? If he is a wicked man?"

"If your interview goes well, he might give you the rec-ommendation you're looking for, that is all—it does not mean that you are his. You can apply within the Citadel to various occupations, and even cross train before and after you choose a specialty; but first you must have a recom-mendation. Once that hurdle is passed then you must stand before the Oracle, a sort of committee of admissions."

Suzie sighed.

Gimcrack and Thiery stopped talking and looked at her.

"I miss Oded." Though she left it unspoken, it seemed she meant to say, 'We ought to find him.'

Lunace, Ogre, and Goblin

Oded tried to think, but it just wasn't easy for him. His twin brother Ubaldo was a good thinker, a right good thinker, only he was deaf, so that made Oded their speaker by default.

Oded glanced at Ublado's fingers to see what he thought. The massive brutes facing them noticed his eyes shift.

"What are you up to?" Lunace growled. He was their leader; worse yet, he was a Cahna-Baal. And he was mean, meaner than the other two: Ogre and Goblin. The brothers had to get away from them, but they'd been looking for an opportunity all night and into the morning. They had missed their meeting with Lord McDougal and every minute made the trail of Suzie's captors colder.

The night had not been easy either. The giants made a pretense of keeping them at their camp as guests, but Oded and Ubaldo had kept their own watch during the night. Alternating watches every few hours, knowing what would happen if they both fell asleep.

Earlier that evening, an hour before sunset, Oded had found the tracks near the Hradcanny high-way; tracks that told the story of a struggle, and horses following the trail not long after. Three horses, two were mounted, most likely McDougal and Fergus.

Some men could read trail as if they were pages in a book. It was the only kind of reading that Oded was good at; in fact he was exceptionally good at it. So they had followed.

Just before coming upon them, the brothers had sent Griz and Woolly—Oded's Grizzly Bear and Ubaldo's warmammoth—into the forest, to be called upon in case they were needed. Oded occasionally saw or heard signs of them during the night, but they had not come in yet, wary of the strangers. They would likely keep their distance.

Oded tried to think of what to do or say. Their antagonists stood over twelve feet tall, muscles bulging; chests and shoulders stood out in such massive proportions as to seem quite unnatural. He could see in their faces and actions that they meant to do evil, but there was also a hesitant squint about the eyes. Though Oded and Ubaldo were three feet shorter than the giants, they were still formidable opponents. The giants had also displayed a strange uneasiness about Ubaldo's deafness and stoic appearance—almost superstitious.

Whatever struggle had taken place yesterday, it had not gone well for the giants. They were bruised, cut, and during the night the left side of Goblin's face had swollen so that his left eye could not open. Lunace was the most dangerous though, and if a fight began, he must be taken down first. Ogre carried a tree limb studded with iron spikes; one blow from that weapon, and a man would surely not survive it. He too limped and grimaced at every step.

But the greatest trouble before them was what Ubaldo called the 'net of evil desire' or sometimes the 'net of wickedness'. Evil men could lay a net or trap, take, kill, and cruelly destroy without hesitation, doing violence against their God given conscience so that it lay wounded and dying within their breast; for even the tender mercies of the wicked are cruel, and the counsels of the wicked are deceit. While the brothers, and honest men like them, could not raise a hand against these giants until the giants' hands were first raised against them; the wicked were not restrained by the high laws of God, and could strike upon a whim.

Oded thought he saw Ubaldo's fingers moving, and so he tried, unsuccessfully to see what counsel his brother was trying to give him—yet without seeming to do so.

"Why do you keep looking at him like that?" Lunace growled again.

"He's talking." Oded tried not to say too much. Ubaldo told him to use very few words, as few as he could; and think real hard before saying them.

The giants stared at Ubaldo, tense. Where Oded wore his thoughts clearly on his face, Ubaldo's expressions were wooden and subtle. When he was signing however, his lips, eyebrows, and his general countenance moved passionately, adding to the meaning of his fingers.

His dead gaze seemed to take in everything, yet be affected by nothing. The giants looked a little alarmed.

"What do you mean he's talking? I thought you said he can't hear or speak."

Oded paused and thought very hard of how to explain sign language with as few words as possible. He kept up a constant repetition in his brain of Ubaldo's instructions to use as few words as possible ... as few words as possible.

"His fingers talk." Oded spoke the words slowly.

The giants, in unison, leaned back. Their eyes narrowed.

The white of Goblin's one good eye widened like a castle moat bloating after a heavy rain; it fastened on Ubaldo's fingers, while he whispered a question directed at Oded, "What do the fingers say?"

Ubaldo began to speak his finger-talk, his sign language.

The big, lumbering, oaken giants leaned forward.

"I don't hear anything."

Oded spoke, deliberate... as few words as possible, "You can't hear it."

Goblin's eye narrowed now, suspicious, "That's what I said."

"Yes, you did." Oded narrowed his eyes in return, not sure why, but it felt like the right thing to do.

The giants looked at one another, and leaned towards the brothers as if they were on the verge of attacking.

Ubaldo began moving his fingers again.

The giants leaned back.

They turned their heads slightly as if they were straining to listen.

Again Goblin spoke, but he sounded more confident now, "I don't think he really is saying anything."

"Yes he is. You just can't hear it." Oded didn't like to have anyone imply that he or his brother were lying.

"Okay then," Lunace interjected, "What's he saying?"

"Well, first he said the words of the wicked are to lie in wait for blood."

"What's that supposed to mean?" Goblin asked, balling his big hand into a fist.

"I don't know."

Lunace scratched his tonsured head. "Goblin, Ogre, come here." The three of them backed away, circled beyond the coals of the fire, and stood in conference just beyond hearing. They all kept their eyes upon the brothers, and so Ubaldo was able to read their lips tolerably well and then relay the conversation to Oded.

Lunace began, "I can't figure them out. Either Oded is really dumb or really smart."

"I think he might be a genius," Ogre said.

"Yeah," added Goblin, "we've already been tricked once by that Rumploony oaf and his lord. We thought they were stupid, but they were just pretending. Made fools of us is what they did."

"So why are these two pretending the deaf one's hands can speak?" Lunace asked.

"Maybe just to confuse us," Ogre said. "You know, keep us off balance."

Suddenly Goblin's one good eye grew large again. "What if he's making incantations? Look at him now—his fingers are definitely doing something, and look how his face moves."

"Yeah," agreed Ogre, "that's kind of weird. He's barely moved a muscle on his face up till now. I bet if we were to turn our backs he'd be winking and smiling at his brother, making fun of us."

Ubaldo smiled and winked.

The giants jumped back.

Goblin was the first to speak, "He can hear us."

Ogre laughed nervously, "What are you talking about, he's deaf."

"Not if he can hear us."

Lunace interrupted, "You fools, even if he wasn't deaf, we're too far away for him to hear us. It must have been a coincidence."

Goblin pulled an idol from his pouch and held it before him like a shield—a shield only a mouse could use. "Maybe he has other ways to hear us. Maybe we should just leave these two alone. I don't like this."

"What?" Lunace threw up his arms. "And be bested two days in a row. I think not."

Lunace marched back around the fire, and stood before the brothers once again. Goblin and Ogre hung back some.

Just then, Ubaldo's face grew intent; he focused on some trees near the cliff edge, signed excitedly, and pointed towards the cliffs.

Now the giants' eyes narrowed to slits, and the color rose in their faces. Not one would turn around to see what Ubaldo pointed at. "We'll not fall for that one again, will we men?" Lunace grit his teeth as he said it.

They answered with gritting teeth of their own.

"So what's your brother trying to say now?" Lunace laughed.

"He said Birdie is over there."

"You must think we're pretty stupid to fall for a dumb trick like that. There are birds all over this forest." Lunace laughed again. Ogre and Goblin laughed with him, sounding forced; they still kept their distance.

Oded held up his hand and whistled. Lunace flinched.

Suddenly, Birdie was perched upon his finger.

At the same moment, Ubaldo gave a high-pitched sound half way between a grunt and the blowing of a horn. It caused the giants to jump. Ogre and Goblin took a step back, and then another step as they heard something coming through the forest.

From the woods came a remarkable sight. Woolly lumbered up to Ubaldo, slowly swinging his trunk, his eleven-foot tusks curved and menacing. But what gave the scene its flavor of the supernatural was Griz riding atop Woolly's shoulders. A thing that the brothers had taught them since Griz was just a cub. But to the superstitious giants it looked like something else altogether.

Oded asked, "Weather, Birdie?"

The giants jumped again. Their own traipsing in the occult would set their minds to imagine every evil specter and other-worldly reckoning for what they were seeing. Talking fingers, Ubaldo's timely wink and smile, a grizzly bear riding upon a mammoth, a man speaking with birds; the fear of it was beating down their pride and courage. Yes, they were wavering.

There was a growing gap between Lunace and his men. As Ogre and Goblin began to retreat, their faces displayed unabashed horror.

Lunace, who was only a few feet from the bird, tilted his head slightly, as though listening to the sound of Ogre and Goblin's footsteps getting further away.

Birdie preened her feathers and then responded clear and sure, "Pretty day."

That did it.

Ogre and Goblin practically tripped over each other as they recoiled and fled.

Lunace was not far behind.

Buried

He opened his eyes, and there was only black; no shades of grey; no dim sense of shadow. No light whatsoever. He thought that he must be in the caves, possibly in Tump Barrows; and his fire, or the lamp must have gone out. Those were the only places he'd experienced such dark—within the caves.

But his mind was all a-swim.

He tried to grasp at something, some memory or thought that would explain.

What was it that was happening?

There it was; that was something anyway. He knew that he was a man who liked to know. Yes, he was a scholar.

Then the shame came pouring upon him, for next he knew that he was a child of the living God. But that was only the second thought that had come to him—not the first, as it should have been. He smiled then in that dark pit where he lay, quick to call out in remembrance that the Lord takes pleasure in them that fear Him, in those that hope in His mercy.

Fear God, yes. But rely upon, seek, and receive His mercy also.

Staffsmitten was a man who loved to meditate upon the grace and mercy of His Lord, and therefore was always quick to run into His arms.

But where am I Lord? I am almost afraid to move or speak.

As of yet, Staffsmitten had not tried to open his mouth, and when he did, only groaning drooled forth. To his own ears, he sounded like some foaming priest of the Bachus or Baal cults, serving nightmares and horrors to their flocks.

His heart beat fast. A wave of feeling in his stomach suddenly lurched toward his chest; his throat seemed tight, constricted. It was difficult to breathe.

O Lord, what has happened to me? I must confess that I am afraid.

Where was he? How had he gotten here?

Nothing came to mind. Nothing that he could grasp—not yet. But there were flickerings of things at the edges of his knowing, trying to run the routes that led to the place where memories could be taken up, played through, and understood.

The flickerings were tantalizing, yet dim and evasive as he tried to catch hold of them. But as soon as he gave up the chase, fear was there to weigh against him. Staffsmitten was not one given to fear, but the tidings of his mind shouted that great evil had befallen him, gotten him, dragged him into this pit. His own mind bespoke evil tidings that scared him to his core.

Then one of those flickerings struggled into familiar form, and Staffsmitten remembered something. He remembered the many times that he poured over the words of God, and how they comforted him. Yes, the Word of God would be a lamp unto his feet, to lighten his darkness; and fear would not have dominion over him. For Staffsmitten was one of those who knew God, knew His Word, and was exercised thereby.

The words to chase away the fear: 'He shall not be afraid of evil tidings: his heart is fixed, trusting in the Lord.'

Staffsmitten lay on his back and he could feel his hands at rest, crossed upon his chest, like those of dead people he'd seen before burial, carefully positioned within their coffin. He disliked the image, and so he strained to move them. The exertion produced another eerie groan from his lips, but his hands gave way from each other, slid along his shirt and down to his legs, but there they were arrested in their progress. He had expected them to fall to his sides and rest upon the surface beneath him, but now he realized that something was pushing in against both his shoulders, and whatever it was had kept his hands from finishing their descent.

His little fingers on each hand wiggled, he brushed the ground below him with their tips—not ground, but wood—he lay upon bare wood. His palms were turned inward toward his legs, and the backs of his hands leaned against another surface—more wood. Now he could smell it, freshly cut.

The image reared its ugly head once more; dead people lying within their coffins. Again the eerie groans, more violent this time, burst from him, as he raised one arm to reach above. He hoped that his fingers would find nothing to touch. But before he had gotten very far, his knuckles struck more wood. It was not the reverberating sound of hollow space beyond it either, but the dull thunk of a solid mass. The weight of earth is what he imagined to be pressing upon it. In any event, he had no strength to push against the surface, and not even enough room to maneuver his body behind the thrust if he did.

Staffsmitten lay within a coffin. A coffin likely buried in the earth.

While he knew now why his breathing was labored, he still could not remember or grasp how it was he came to be there. Why did his head swim so? Why was there no strength in his limbs? And why could he not utter normal speech?

Yet, Staffsmitten had been exercised by the Word of God. He would no longer dread the evil tidings that had befallen him, shrink in fear, or be anxious for God's deliverance. Should he dishonor his heavenly Father with such thoughts?

He hoped not. With God's grace, he would wait upon the LORD. He would do as Job had done, and accept whatever God would give him—life or death—and God would get the glory.

Peace that passeth all understanding calmed his nerves for duty to God, and sustained his languishing body against the trial before him.

It was still black; there was no light at all. No way of escape.

But Staffsmitten's soul soared.

Meanwhile, in the valley of Hradcanny, Mamma lay in a similar stupor.

She and the others had tried to fight, and help the man-thing. But the bright-shinies had filled the air and struck; sharp bites that did not hurt terribly, but they did madden her, and the hot rage of battle swept over her body.

The young skunks spewed out their noxious stink as they too were hit by the bright-shinies. The nearest of the clan were spattered with skunk spray; those which were most affected bolted into the woods. But they did not make it far.

Mamma had rushed forward to maul the nearest hound and rider. Suddenly her limbs felt heavy. When the hound stepped sideways, she tried to turn; forelimbs folding beneath her, she slumped to the ground. Her eyelids closed against her will, and then even sound ceased.

Throughout the next day, she came in and out of sleep; sun warmed her fur. Occasionally she would hear the approaching paws of predators. They would stay but a minute and then wander away. The last time though, she was able to open her eyes; she could feel her strength returning, yet not enough to pull herself up.

There was a footfall just behind her head; a nudge against her neck. The most Mamma could do was a piteous growl.

A pause; then there was sniffing at her ear so that the sound multiplied greatly. Mamma gave another growl, this one was slightly louder, and a fiercer rumble pressed out through her exposed teeth and curved lip. Another pause, then the padded feet came across her line of vision.

A panther, sniffing, sniffing, and cautious, tread among them. Its pink nose wrinkling. No doubt it disliked the strong scent of man about the clearing, and worse, the pungent reek of skunk; but some of the clan had escaped direct contact with it, and over one of these the panther now hung his head.

The little fox, whose sibling had been buried just yesterday, lay motionless under the panther's stare.

No, not the fox kit. She would not let her young one be taken without a struggle. Mamma growled again. A rush of brutal anger and she was on her feet. She felt sunken, sick, and her body trembled.

The panther nudged the fox over onto its back, limp. There was no sign of life. None that Mamma could see. But her vision was blurred. She staggered, tried to take a step, and yet failed to move forward. She looked to the ground to steady her feet, and fought with equal fury against its beckoning force that commanded her to give in, fall to its grassy embrace, and rest the wobbling motion of her legs.

When she next raised her eyes, the big cat was exiting the clearing as a prince of animals leaving his royal domain—his back was to the clan, his tail swept the air with a lazy sway—the beast was poised, handsome, and glorious.

Mamma turned her blurry gaze back to her young one.

The Fox kit was gone.

Grave Robbers

Thiery noticed Gimcrack switch to another chair. It seemed a strange thing to do, until he saw that Horatio was sitting near the just vacated seat. It suddenly became clear.

Thiery must have worn his understanding on his face, for he looked at Gimcrack, and was met with a proud chin and color in the dwarf's cheeks.

Suzie noticed too. "Gimcrack, sir, are you afraid of Horatio?" It was an innocent question that could only have come from her compassionate heart, but they were painful and unpleasant words for the hearer.

The color in his face deepened. He first inclined towards anger, clenched his fist, rose from his seat and spoke somewhat harshly. "Afraid? Of course I'm not ..."

Suzie's wide eyes stopped his speech.

He began again, his tone tempered, even tender. "I'm sorry, little one. I don't like the word is all. From 'afraid' men's minds hear 'coward'. I like to think of myself as cautious. Now that has a pleasant ring to me." He looked from Suzie to Thiery with his eyes raised, his head tilted, as if questioning them, cautiously determining if his assertion was meeting with any support.

They both smiled.

"You see," Gimcrack continued, encouraged. "Horatio is a wild animal, only recently begun to be tamed. And as I would like to keep myself from being bitten in a moment when his wildness asserts itself over his tameness, I think it more comfortable, nay, even wise, to sit over here." He looked pleased with his discourse until his eyes fell upon Thiery. "You hide not your frown very well young man."

"I mean no disrespect, sir, it's just ..."

"Out with it then."

"You are our elder, a friend to us, and many times you have saved us with great ability and courage. We greatly esteem you, sir."

"But ..." Gimcrack prompted, obviously pleased by the speech.

"It is just this, sir. We look to you as our guide and counselor. In fact, it is due to your counsel that I hope for a second interview tomorrow with Master Squilby. I had an idea of how some things might be arranged, and not wanting to be too forward in my opinion, was looking for a way to broach a certain subject. Now I find it even more difficult to bring up. And therefore you have seen me frown, sir."

"Again I say, out with it. As your elder, guide, and counselor then, I give you a favorable wind to share your thoughts."

"Thank you, sir. I will proceed boldly then. Horatio has taken a protective liking to Suzie. I find this most desirable to encourage, seeing that you and I must be looking for work. This leaves Suzie here in Old City, sometimes with neither you nor I as company and protection. Horatio can be an excellent companion and guard for my sister."

Suzie giggled and clapped her hands ever so quietly, though bursting with energy that found an outlet in her small bodied, yet big squirming antics. She volunteered her thoughts when Thiery paused to look at her. "Sorry. I didn't mean to interrupt. I just like it when you call me your sister. Please continue my … brother … my big brother." She giggled again and sat on her hands.

"As you see, sir, she is a treasure."

"Yes, indeed she is, but why do you hesitate to share these thoughts that you must have known I hardily agree with."

They had called her a treasure.

Suzie's smile had now grown to magnificent proportions. Her eyes sparkled; joy and adoration exuded from every part of her being—a contented sigh, the tilt of her head, multiplied dimples. Thiery laughed to see that look directed at himself and Gimcrack, and knew there could be no better time to press forward.

"I know that we should like to keep our home here somewhat of a secret. It's easy enough to access the larger streets from many different paths, why, we could even go through the temple grounds or the grave-yard to vary our approach so as not to draw attention. But, what about Horatio? He stands out, and he only grows larger.

"So, I thought we could take him out before the sun rises and after it sets. Rarely will we need to bring him out during the day. I say 'we', but Suzie cannot be on the streets after dark. Of course, I am his trainer, and take the responsibility as such."

"Of course." Gimcrack had begun to look alarmed at the use of the word we.

"But..." Thiery continued.

"But? There need not be a but," Gimcrack blurted. "It all seems quite clear."

"It's just that, sir, there may be times that I will be unavailable. Who knows what my duties may be, and while Horatio is still young it would be good for him to know that you are wolf-in-command. By taking him out at times, and leading him about, it will show him that you are to be respected, sir." Leading, commanding, and receiving respect were words that Thiery saw had a modifying effect on Gimcrack.

"Hmmm, I don't know. I see some advantages to your arguments, but a wise and cautious man needs time to think."

Suzie chimed in, her eyes filled with wonder. "Oh, Gimcrack, sir, you would be so striking as wolf-in-command. I really like the sound of that. Don't you think that sounds wonderful? Wolf-in-command! Oh my, what a picture that puts in my head!"

"I suppose it has a certain ring to it."

"Oh, yes, it does," Suzie gasped. "You fight serpents, you fight several wicked priests all by yourself, you fight dragons, you save young maidens, you help foundlings, and now you are to be a wolf-in-command." By the end of her oration she was standing upon her chair; Thiery too had risen to his feet, and Gimcrack had drawn his mace above his head slashing at invisible foes.

"Yes," Gimcrack said, with his chest inflated and his voice deep, "there is a time for caution and a time for action. Now is the time for action; I will be a wolf-in-command. Thiery, my boy, show me what to do."

An hour of instruction passed by, the sun was sufficiently set, and the moon sufficiently risen. Gimcrack slid a secret stone, just under the stair, and out they went, emerging behind a thick hedge. Thiery carried a heavy quarterstaff, gifted to him from Gimcrack, compliments of the Dwarven Brotherhood. Gimcrack thought it a more suitable weapon to carry in the city than a bow.

"Almost, sir," Thiery whispered, "but you must keep in front of him, don't let him direct you."

Gimcrack grunted his assent. "He's overly large, Thiery."

"Yes, give a snap on his lead or turn when he begins to overtake you. That's the way of it, sir."

"I grow dizzy with all this turning. Is there not an easier way to be wolf-in-command?"

"Maybe he is somewhat bored with this small court; you could take him into the grave-yard. There is a wide green not yet filled with graves or crypts, a path that wanders through and around the edges, and there's not much chance of encountering people in there at night."

Gimcrack flinched. "I should say not. And there's not much chance of encountering me in there, day or night."

Thiery laughed. "You wouldn't need to go near the burial places, sir. And it would give you a longer circuit to practice with. Besides, now that you're a child of the living God, you have nothing to fear from spirits and such."

Gimcrack didn't answer, but instead leaned his head around the corner of wall that separated them from the grave-yard beyond. He studied the place for minutes, turning his head at the slightest sounds. "It's not an altogether terrible looking place, but you'll have to admit there is an eerie quality that lurks about it. But, do you know young man, it seems to be working."

"What is that, sir?"

"Those Words of God ... that Job wrote down, the ones you helped me memorize this morning. They really do help give me a peace: 'For his eyes are upon the ways of man, and seeth all his goings. There is no darkness, nor shadow of death, where the workers of iniquity may hide themselves.'

So, according to that, He can see us right this moment. Isn't that right, my boy?"

"It is indeed, sir."

"And I shouldn't like to seem the coward, or should I say overly cautious, before my LORD."

"No, sir."

"I can tell you, for you already know my greatest fears—water, and losing my way in the dark caverns with no light to guide me, and maybe one or two more things—but the burial places of the dead have always been a close third for me. I don't believe I've ever set foot in one, at least not at night. Do you think God would be well pleased with me if I would go in there with this here wolf?"

"He takes not pleasure in the legs of a man," Thiery replied. "He's pleased, sir, if when you go in there, that you fear Him, and hope in His mercy. Blessed is that man that makes the LORD his trust."

"Well, I'll have no trouble fearing Him, and I suppose it is easier to hope in His mercy than to prove myself a worthy fellow."

"Yes, sir, certainly none of us can prove ourselves worthy before Him."

Gimcrack seemed to flounder between his thoughts of dread and thoughts of God. "I'm just not sure. There are other things to consider. Look at that entrance on the far side over there. The wall is high, if someone should come that way, we'd not have much warning. And there's no crowd to blend in with."

"I'll take care of that, sir." Thiery shot across the grass, and jumped, just grasping the wall's summit. He pulled himself up, and laid on his belly, a still, quiet sentry. There wasn't anyone to be seen on the far side, and so Thiery motioned that the way was clear.

After a few minutes hesitation, Gimcrack reached one foot out before him, touching the ground, but not resting any weight upon it. It struck Thiery as being familiar … yes, he had seen the very same behavior among children; ready to plunge into a cold pond, first they would touch it lightly with their toes, shivering with delight. Only Gimcrack hadn't any delightedness about him.

But following his toe-full inspection, Gimcrack too, jumped in, a tense figure, rapt with head jerking wariness, moving along the grassy yard at a terribly brisk pace. Once in, he was making a bold circuit of the grounds, glancing at Thiery as he passed under him. A nervous, almost panicked smile frozen to his face; his upper teeth protruded as he drew his lips back and curled them up under his nose.

His second circumambulation seemed slightly better. He was loosening up, and this time only Gimcrack's right lip, right cheek, and right eyebrow were raised stiffly—his mouth partly open. Yet still, somehow his upper teeth seemed to stick forward like a rabbit about to chew—this being the more relaxed of his panicky smiles. After Gimcrack passed,

Thiery looked quickly into the alley from which he was supposed to keep watch, but only quickly, for he didn't want to miss anything on the more interesting side.

Gimcrack never made it a third time around.

Without warning, Horatio lowered his nose to the ground, extended his paws and legs at an angle that anchored him against forward thrust, and shifted his weight back. Gimcrack came to a sudden stop.

Gimcrack's head snapped and wobbled in every direction trying to take in the cause of the abrupt change. Horatio turned abruptly and was off; Gimcrack's arm was jerked along with the lead in his hands, and before he could prevent it, he was pulled amidst the graves and yawning crypts. He almost gained his footing, when his arm brushed against a stone sepulcher; he danced and swatted at that side of his body like a thing gone mad.

The struggle, while furious, was hushed, not a peep dared escape from Gimcrack. Then, a voice, or more like a groan, carried up from the graves as if from under the earth itself.

Gimcrack froze, quivering; a moan escaped from his belly.

As if in answer, another groan from under foot pealed forth yet again.

Horatio's head tilted a questioning look at the dark earth, and he then fell to digging with wild, powerful abandon. The dirt flew in the air and sprayed against Gimcrack in a constant torrent—within seconds a pile was quickly burying his legs. Buried in a grave-yard … with dead people … at night … in the dark. Still he did not move.

Thiery hadn't expected anything like this; he thought that he must abandon his post and aid his friend, and stop the unthinkable thing that Horatio was doing. But he had been so consumed by the amazing scene before him, that he had already fallen short of his duty as sentry.

Low chanting brought him back. He had raised himself up on his elbows, but now he slowly laid his cheek along the stones, hugging the top of the wall, and prayed that he had not been seen. There was a familiar sound to those chants. An icy chill closed about his heart—Dragon Priests.

There were half a score of them, robed and hooded. They were entering the alley and coming towards him, only fifty paces away. Would they just pass by the grave-yard, continuing through the city streets, stirring fear in the breasts of those who slept and those that cowered within their lodgings? Or would they be drawn to this place of graves? Or worse, did they intend to come here for some frightful purpose? In such a large city, how could it be that they were here, almost close enough to reach out and touch? How would Gimcrack react?

A moan lifted to his place upon the wall. The priests didn't seem to notice as they droned on. But they were getting closer, and they might hear it yet. They paused very near to where he lay, and raised their arms. The chanting ceased. One of the priests called out in a babbled tongue, the others responded in a cadenced voice of assent.

A moment of silence.

Another priest called out, alone.

The others called back.

Another moment of silence—this time it was broken by a moan, carried up again from the grave near Gimcrack. It was faint. Would the sound of it reach the Dragon Priests?

With one accord they slowly turned their hooded heads.

Thiery's heart beat so that he feared they might hear its pounding. The portion of wall he lay upon was still concealed in shadow, contrasted against the stones where moonlight reached. Yet those hoods faced his way, and it took all his nerve not to move or even breathe. He could see them clearly, and yet he hoped they could not see him at all. He could only hope, and pray, and wait.

They turned away, chanting again, moving slowly towards the entrance he feared they would turn in at.

As soon as they passed his place upon the wall, Thiery let himself down, and ran towards Gimcrack's trembling form. A pile of dirt now reached to his thighs, but he did nothing to free himself. He just stared into the growing hole before him.

Horatio's paws speedily whirled and scratched. The grave was shallow, and now his claws were scraping loudly upon a wooden coffin, gouging splinters free from the soft pine.

"Someone's coming." Thiery shook Gimcrack's shoulder. He was afraid to tell him that it was not just someone who came, but that it was Dragon Priests, and many of them. Gimcrack stared, his top lip was still curled back and up under his nose, his teeth still protruded unnaturally.

Thiery grabbed Horatio's lead and pulled. Horatio leaned forward and continued to denude the coffin planks.

"Gimcrack, sir, help me please."

His lippy, toothy face gaped at him in reply.

The chanting of the priests suddenly got louder; they must be either passing the opening or coming through. Thiery couldn't spare a moment to look as he wrestled and commanded, yet with whispered words. He finally managed to pull Horatio off the grave and back to a more controlled semblance of mind.

The Dragon Priests were indeed paused at the entrance of the grave-yard. Moonlight glinted against long knives they had drawn from the folds of their robes. They ceased their chanting and peered through.

Gimcrack lowered himself to the earth; Thiery and Horatio crouched at his side.

Whatever it was that caused Horatio to lose his head, he was now behaving well. Not even a growl, just a low rumble vibrated against Thiery's left hand, which he pressed against Horatio's breast. His right hand lay along the wolf's back, and he could feel the ripple of skin and raised hair that bespoke his readiness to fight.

If only the priests would move on. Thiery had stooped in an uncomfortable position, and now normally unused muscles began to ache. But he dared not shift his weight. Even Gimcrack had stopped shaking. Everything was so still. All their attention was riveted upon the hooded forms that skulked nearby. So intense was his concentration, so forceful the growing strain in his legs, that it took a moment to realize something else was happening.

A grunt.

The sound of sand grating.

A clod of dirt fell back into the grave.

Another grunt. Then a slight, sandy, wooden tremble from the hole, only inches from them, yet black within.

There was something down there. Something alive.

The nearness of that shallow grave and the sounds it was emitting brought the quaking back to Gimcrack's limbs. There was an instant rushing sound of sliding sand and clay as the coffin top began to rise on one side, and then rest against the grave's earthen wall. It was dark, but something had pushed it open, something that looked like an arm—with fingers that grasped the top edge.

Then the dark took on further substance as something moaned and grunted, rising to a seated position within the woody grave. Its shape looked vaguely human, and then it slurped out a horrible sound, more of a word than a moan.

"Gee..ee…mm…caaa…akk." One of its arms reached towards them.

Gimcrack's body, again, ceased to quaver.

He fell over, limp, his weight pressing hard against Thiery.

The Priests assuredly heard the unnatural utterance, yet they stood still, their dark hoods gaped towards the place where Theiry and Horatio crouched, and where Gimcrack lay. If he took his arms from Horatio, the wolf might spring into action. Gimcrack was insensible and he would be too heavy for Thiery to move on his own.

Thiery was also conscious of the grip of fear that was holding his own limbs and mind from choosing some path. For now at least, the grave markers, crypts, and above-ground stone vaults kept them hidden. Here and there were rectangular openings in the earth where dark, cold stairs descended into unknown chambers or maybe even catacombs.

The ghoulish figure before them grunted more and began clawing at the earth, it seemed that it was pulling itself out.

The Dragon Priests were moving too, led by the daggers in outstretched arms before them as if they were talismans to ward off danger. Their robes flowed around the graves, and they began to spread out. It would soon be too late to do anything.

Calling on God, Thiery laid Gimcrack softly to the ground, and gripped Horatio's lead tight and close to his body. There was a stone sarcophagus a few feet from them, raised up on pillars, with a dark void beneath it. Thiery pushed against Gimcrack's legs, then shoulders, then legs, then shoulders, speedily stowing him beneath it.

The priests were close. He could hear them in front and behind. There was only one thing to do. Leaving Gimcrack unconscious and hopefully hidden, Thiery pulled Horatio to the nearest hole; they plunged into the dark, down the stairs. Moving rapidly at first, Thiery continued more cautiously when he believed them fully swallowed. He wanted to put distance between himself and the surface in case the priests produced a light. The steps ended after a descent of twenty or so feet.

He reached out to the left and felt nothing, then to the right, and again there was nothing but cool dark air—a room then, or possibly a wide passage. Thiery looked back up the stairs, towards the increasing moans, and frantic clawing sounds of whatever or whoever was emerging from the grave above. At first his view was only a rectangular opening of night sky and stars, but then he saw, first one hand, and then another grip the top stair.

A face, silhouetted against the sky, wobbled and peeked over the edge, resting on the hands that went before it; it seemed that was all it was, a bodiless head ready to roll down and get him. He knew it couldn't be, but all the same it made him terribly afraid. Horatio pulled against the lead, trying to move forward, towards the fearsome sight.

The head began to slide down the steps. Then he could see shoulders and arms; his emotions now agreed with his mind that it was indeed a man that came after him. But why did he slither upon the ground? And why did he make such grotesque sounds? Why did he come up out of a grave? And why was he pursuing Thiery?

Suddenly, Horatio stiffened, his hackles raised. A second later, Dragon Priests loomed over the entrance, pulling the man back. It seemed a blow was struck; there was one more stunted groan, and then silence.

Thiery dared not move. He prayed that Gimcrack would not wake up. Stuffed under a stone coffin as he was, he'd likely panic and possibly scream.

Thiery hugged Horatio, and laid his head against the wolf's warm fur; as he did so, he realized how tired he was. He felt the weariness growing, but his eyes were not heavy, not yet. The adrenaline, the danger, the unknown, it all kept him far from sleep. The priests began moving about; there were hushed words, and then the crunch and slice of shovels digging.

The Interview

Horatio stirred. Thiery opened his eyes; how long they had been shut, he didn't know—yet it was still night. He no longer heard any sounds from the grave-yard, and so, after waiting and listening for ten minutes, he quietly climbed the stairs.

He kept his head just beneath the level of the earth and scanned the stony shapes of crypts and grave markers, and the shadows they made. Next, he watched Horatio for any signs that he might sense danger; but the wolf was calm.

Thiery remembered how Oded had first taught him the lessons of movement within the forest, or wilderness, or any arena really where it was necessary to stay concealed. Waiting could draw out an enemy, but if you must move, to look around a rock or through a leafy wood, then move like the budding of a flower.

Until then, Thiery had only seen flowers in the open or closed position. But Oded set him ten strides from a morning glory and told him to watch. It was excruciatingly slow and difficult to keep his attention riveted to the spot; by the time the flower had fully blossomed, he had occasionally seen diminutive bursts, but there were always the movements and sounds of other things to draw his attention away, to make him unsure of the flower's measured advance. Yet, when Oded finally came for him, there was the bloom, awakened to the morning.

Thiery tried to lift his head above the plane of the earth; carefully, slowly; for long minutes he rose from the inky depth. If the priests were waiting in ambush, they would not likely know in what corner their quarry would be hidden, making it all the more difficult to see slight movements. They could not even know if there really was anyone here. All the same, they may have left at least one man behind; it was obvious that someone had been grave digging.

From this vantage Thiery could see Gimcrack's boot. It was a great relief, for he half expected Gimcrack to have been taken away by the Priests.

Ever so slowly, Thiery turned his head, his eyes moving from boot to shin, to knee, and it seemed like an eternity before he reached the leather belt with a hand laid beside it; he continued to wrist, to elbow, and finally to shoulder. Each body part was unmoving, peaceful, at rest. He was suddenly afraid for Gimcrack; he couldn't see into the recesses of the hiding place, where Gimcrack's chest should be rising and falling with each breath.

Gimcrack's head was rolled to the side, facing the hole where Thiery was concealed, so that both their heads were at the same level, and less than ten feet from each other.

Next he could see the chin, the open mouth, the nose, and then the eyes.

Open eyes. Wide open.

They blinked, and got wider still.

Gimcrack's lips once again peeled back, scrunching under his nose, and those big teeth protruded like a donkey.

"It's me." Thiery whispered.

"Thiery?"

"That's right, sir. And Horatio's with me."

"Why can't I see anything but the top of your head?"

"Dragon Priests came, so I pushed you under that … that … stone, and I hid down these stairs. But I'm not sure if they're still around."

Gimcrack crawled out from under the crypt, and shuddered when he saw what it was. Thiery and Horatio joined him, all three crouching in the shadows.

"Look!" Gimcrack pointed to the open grave; where the groaning man had reached for them; now there was its twin a few feet farther to the right—yet both were mere holes in the ground, no coffins. "What could this mean? It's a beastly business, Thiery." Then Gimcrack looked into the night sky. "I'll be," he said, "it's almost morning, yes, I'm sure of it. Look how the moon has disappeared beyond the buildings there. In ten minutes you'll be seeing morning on its way. Which means, you'll be late."

Thiery had completely forgotten about his appointment with Master Squilby. He would have to hurry. "Poor Suzie, sir, she must be in an awful fright wondering what's happened to us. Can you take Horatio, and comfort Suzie? I'll hurry back. Tell her she'll be in my prayers."

"Do be careful, my boy, for this night's happenings have shaken me something awful, and I'll not feel right again till you're back, safe with us. There's something here that I feel I should place my finger upon, but I'm all a jitter, and to be honest I'm flabby-aghast. My mind's become simpleton mush.

"Better be off with you now. I'll be praying and reciting those God-words till my mind's better suited to think on these things. Up with you now, run like the wind. I'll see to Suzie."

"God bless you, Gimcrack, sir."

"God bless you, boy."

Thiery ran through the streets and alleys, aware that some might think him an easy target. The pickpockets, thieves, and worse, would likely be bold with the cover of darkness. Yet his mind was preoccupied with what Gimcrack and he had just witnessed. Who was that man? Why had the Dragon Priests come to get him? Was he with them, or was he trying to get away from them? Why had Horatio dug him up? Just mere curiosity? And why were there two open graves? Surely then the priests had intended all along to come and do some digging of their own.

Soon his thoughts were dragged away from the mystery, for the nearer he came to the citadel's walls, winding up the narrow streets of the old city, the more he noted the eyes. Eyes on the streets, in windows, peering from alleys—each set with indistinct shapes attached to them. One pair of eyes from the shadows of a hooded cloak were soft and friendly. Some were bright, lit with curiosity. Some dim, barely apparent. Some, furrowed, red and yellow veined.

And there was one which he raced to meet, deep set in a hollowed socket, lined with grime; it had leaned forward through a three-inch by three-inch peephole just yesterday. That was the eye Thiery was hurrying to meet with now. The voice behind the eye, that of Master Squilby, had told him, "Be back tomorrow before the sun's rays hit the top most tower of the citadel."

It was dark, barely so, and yet people were about. Thiery saw their eyes in the pre-morning mist that was moving in off the bog lands. He studied them, especially those that looked his way and lingered. The first time he had come here, it seemed that no one took any notice of him, but now it seemed that others were watching, gauging him, maybe even following him.

He was alone with the shapes in the shadows. Still he pressed on towards the interview and the door with the three-inch by three-inch peep.

He pushed his toes against the leather of his boots, gripping each cobblestone as he passed under the outer court's gate. Something moved in the upper periphery of his vision. He looked up to the solitary gatehouse window. A hand reached out and tapped a knife against the half raised portcullis with a rhythm that seemed to match Theiry's step.

He paused at the thought and the tapping ceased.

Thiery stared up at the window. There was no face in its recess, just a hand poised to strike an iron bar. Thiery slowly raised his foot and set it back down.

Tap.

The muscles in his back and neck began to tighten. Then, peering into the courtyard beyond, he was drawn towards the iron bound door. Though he could not see the hole from this distance—it was cloaked by fog and a darkness that was just lightly intruded upon—he could remember its unusual location only a few feet from the ground, and the sound that the metal peep cover had made, scraping as it slid open.

And then he heard it; the peep was moving—a sound that pierced the fog, and rasped upon his teeth; a sound that both repulsed and beckoned him forward. And Master Squilby waited beyond it.

The courtyard was illuminated by a single torch whose meager light danced over the empty space—empty except for a group of boys about Thiery's age. Talking quietly among themselves, they whittled at some wood, and cast an occasional glance his way; strange that they should be so occupied at that early hour.

Thiery moved forward again. One whittler tapped his knife against the stones. The beat matched Thiery's step.

Theiry forced his fingers to relax upon his heavy quarterstaff, and with his free hand he loosened the leather thong against his dagger's hilt. With each step, the dagger jiggled in its too large scabbard. Feeling vulnerable and unsure, Thiery made a pretense of letting his staff fall to the ground.

Bending to pick it up, he glanced back at the gate, the street, and the inn beyond.

At the street, a green hooded cloak sank deeper into shadow. And from inside the tavern, a single candle illuminated a bearded face. The beard twitched, and the candlelight snuffed. Rising, Thiery walked the remaining steps to the door.

What would unfold? So many watching, straining at the impending interview. But why? Thiery bent awkwardly forward and looked into the open peephole. The bulging eye of Squilby was there, made bright by the dirt surrounding it.

"Good Morning, sir," Thiery said.

"Good, hah, not much good about it. Tell me lad, what is good about this morning?"

Thiery glanced at the boys nearby as he tried to think.

"They'll not give you an answer. Quick now, tell me. Or is it as I say, a miserable day like every other?"

"I think it very good, sir, that I made it here safe and ..."

"I suppose," Squilby interrupted, chuckling behind the door. "Unless you are one of the many who are out to cut your throat and rob your purse."

Thiery forced a smile at the strange humor and looked back over his shoulder.

"Why so nervous boy? Do you imagine the cutthroats at your back?"

"No, sir," he answered. "It's just that, well, it seems that I'm being watched."

"Of course you're being watched, we were expecting you." His eyebrow rose slightly.

"Yes, sir."

"Tell me boy, who is watching you? Where do they watch you from? Leave nothing out."

"Those boys." Thiery nodded his head slightly in their direction. "And the man at the gate house ..."

"Natural enough," Squilby said. "I thought you bold to travel the city through darkness, but maybe you're just foolish and afraid of your own shadow."

"No, sir," Thiery said, struggling with his own pride. "Also there was a man in a green cloak near the tavern, and another man inside it. I believe the one with the cloak held a weapon at the ready. Maybe a bow."

"Boy," Squilby said, with his eyebrow slanting down, and his tone different, "slowly, take one step to the side, and do not turn around." Thiery obeyed, watching as a thick blackened finger pushed against the ballooning eye, its shape now grossly elongated. Straining through the mist, it seemed the ball would tear from its socket, fall from its perch within the peep, and roll into the street for a better view.

"Nothing. I can't see a darn thing... yet to be sure," Squilby whispered. Then he gave a commanding snort, "Pip!" The eyeball snapped back as the finger disappeared from view.

Then, a wink of motion, and a wiry boy stood at Thiery's side. "Pip, at your service, Master Squilby..." Realizing some mistake, the last word drifted away awkwardly.

"Oh, Pip, not good." The eye rolled back, until only the white, striped with veins, emerged. "A blunder Pip, one that makes me sick, a maggot stenching blunder."

Transfixed by the eye, Pip's body wriggled like a freshly caught fish, then wilted in his captor's grasp.

Squilby's voice squeezed out his name. "Pip, what if our guest did not know my name? How many times must I tell you not to use my name when in the company of strangers? Should you decide when my name is to be given?" Pip's head shot back and forth. His lips constricted to a blue-purple. "Okay then, here is your chance to erase this blunder from my memory."

"Oh, yes, Master..., sir, um..," Pip seemed to struggle with what to replace his master's name. His body began a slight vibration, when from his mouth burst forth, "Pip, at your service, and erase it I will."

"Good. Listen closely: tavern, Witchum Street, alley," then a long pause. Pip leaned forward, holding up three fingers, when Squilby said, "Reconnoiter." Pip stared blankly, teetering upon his toes.

"Oh, Pip!" Once again Squilby's eye rolled grotesquely back. "That word is on the list, it means to spy out an area." Recognition snapped over Pip's features, and then he was gone as suddenly as he had appeared.

"On we go then," Squilby said, looking again at Thiery. "Tell me, yesterday you said you'd like to be a ranger. Why? Don't you know that of all the certainties you can find of a certain, for certain rangers die? They usually die soon, and they die in a bad way. Do you want to die boy?"

"I don't, sir."

"Good, then let me tell you some of the other trades of which you can choose here at the Citadel. For the adventurous there are beast trainers of which I am headmaster." Here he paused and squinted. "You like the beasts, don't you, boy?"

"I do, sir, very much."

"And you have a special affection for dogs and wolves and such, yes?"

"Yes, sir."

"You even have one?"

"Yes, sir." Thiery was startled. What else did Master Squilby know about him?

"Hah, don't look so surprised, it's easy enough to see. First off, there aren't many boys who don't like animals, and I figured by the way you're covered with animal hair, that it was a dog; in fact you've got so much on you that you likely have been sleeping with it.

"Anyway, there's more to choose from yet, there are sneaks such as Pip and these other boys, though you may be a bit large for that, and men-at-arms. Or there are mapmakers who must venture beyond the city and so they also often die prematurely. And for the scholarly, there are much safer pursuits from which you may choose. For instance, there are scribes, interpreters, engineers, astronomers, alchemists, apothecaries and others. Would you like to hear more, or does anything I've described so far command your interest?"

"With all respect, sir," Thiery replied, and uncomfortable from looking down, dropped to one knee, "It is my dream to be a ranger."

"As I was afraid of. Without looking, tell me how many boys sit whittling over there."

"There are five, not counting Pip."

"Good." Squilby whistled, and the boys came; some ran, some tumbled, and some flipped through the air. In a moment they stood round Thiery. "Sneaks, give me his measurements." A number of the boys produced measuring lines and began to stretch them about Thiery's body, calling out as they went, "height: five feet ten inches", "biceps", "chest", "legs". One of the larger boys grabbed Thiery in a bear hug and lifted him from the ground, "weight: about one fifty." Then they stepped back at attention leaving Thiery tousled.

"You show some promise for growing into a tall man, and powerfully built." Squilby seemed to spit the words out, and then his eye closed to a slit, and his voice, for the first time sounded happy. "Have you been in any fights? Do you know how to use that quarterstaff?"

"A few, sir, and I know the basics I think."

"Good. What if you were to die? Are you afraid to die boy?" Squilby's eye sparkled.

"No, sir."

"Are you that good then, or is it that the gods you worship are so powerful?"

"Neither, sir, I worship the one true God, and if I fight well, then He has helped me, and if I die, then to Him I will go." Thiery sensed the boys around him stiffen.

"My favored god is Marduk." There was a hint of something dangerous to Squilby's voice. "And these boys offer to many gods, yet you are one of those who hold to Elohiym, and worse you say that he is the only true God. Will he fight for you?"

"If it's His will, then yes."

"I suppose the odds against you would not matter if in fact your God chose to intervene. Even if—let's just throw a number out there, let's say five against one."

"Yes, sir, He can do anything." Thiery's heart was pounding. He began to pray.

"Excellent!" Squilby sounded almost joyful. "What about a sneak attack? What if your knife had been pilfered?" Thiery slowly reached for his belt and felt his empty scabbard. Looking down, his dagger was gone.

He never saw the blow that crashed against his head.

The Test

Thiery lay sprawled upon the cobbles still clutching his staff. He tried to rise, but the blows from five assailants came quickly—boots, fists, and the butts of knives. Thiery closed in upon himself and prayed.

Almost as soon as it had begun, they stopped. Thiery staggered to his feet, surprised and grateful that he hadn't been too badly hurt.

Dazed, Thiery leaned heavily on his weapon. Was this part of the interview? Was there more to come? Had he failed?

The sneaks now stood beyond the reach of his quarterstaff. He looked from one boy to the next, some averted their gaze, and others glared back defiantly. Squilby chuckled from behind the door.

"Sneaks, let this be a lesson to you." Squilby pounded the door with each word, "Elohiym is not so powerful as the boy would have you believe. But something is seriously wrong, serious indeed. You beat him handily, but I can tell when your heart is not in a thing, and worse, when some of you pretend or weaken a blow. Be sure that I will not forget, and others will hear of your conduct."

Squilby's eye rested upon Thiery who now stood straight, knees slightly bent, and holding his staff at quarter, in guard position.

"What do you say about your God now, boy? He failed you, yes?" Squilby prompted.

A realization came over Thiery as Squilby spoke. He had been persecuted for the name of God. He smiled.

"I offer no disrespect to you, Master Squilby, or to your sneaks. In normal circumstances I would accuse the tactics used against me as dishonorable. But I would like to think that you acted, not dishonorably, but out of a genuine interest in seeing whether or not God would fight for me. If I had won a fair contest, then you would naturally assume I had conquered through my own abilities. But, if I had triumphed against your unfair and ignoble means, you would then know that God had indeed championed my cause. So I take no offense, but if your sneaks get too close again, I'll have to assume the worst and defend myself." Thiery brushed at the sweat trickling down his brow. He pulled his hand away—it was not sweat, but blood.

"Well said, boy, except what you call unfair, I call strategy and surprise. You would do well to take note, guard against it, and employ it yourself. In any event, I gave you more notice than most. But what now are your thoughts on Elohiym? Do you care to insult our gods again by labeling them false?"

"Elohiym is as true as He was before my beating."

"Do you mean to say then that he is the only true God, and other gods are not?"

"I do, sir."

Squilby's fist struck against the door, his eyeball squeezing at the peep. "Are you daft then? If he is so true, why did he not aid you?"

"You put forth a test of your own making, and believed that God would play your game by your rules. Would you automatically obey a similar mandate put forth by one of your students? I don't think you would, and yet you dared test the very Creator of all things and demand that He perform at your pleasure. I do not know why God allowed me to be struck down just now, but His ways are not man's ways, and His ways are often past finding out."

Squilby's eye closed, and a reddish hue bored through the filth. All was quiet. The boys shifted, scratched, and looked at each other with eyebrows raised.

Squilby caressed the silence with a whisper, "I don't like you boy." Then he began to laugh. "But you intrigue me. So I put forth another test. It is one hundred feet between this door and the portcullis. If you can reach the gatehouse then I will give you my endorsement to enroll in our academy. If the sneaks can stop you then no endorsement, and we keep your dagger. Do you agree to the terms?"

"Sir, I did not mean to deceive you when you asked if I could use this weapon, for I was explaining myself as but a youth with much still to learn. And I did not want to boast.

But I must now be more open. For my age, I think I have been trained rather well in the use of it. I tell you this because I am bigger than your sneaks, they are armed only with daggers, and the quarterstaff hasn't many weapons to rival it. I do not wish to win your contest unfairly."

"Most noble of you boy," Squilby said, dripping with sarcasm. "And now, since you have warned us of our certain defeat, I will give you a different assessment with fair warning that all is not as it seems. You are somewhat wounded. You are one against five, and one of your weapons is no longer on your person. I am no fool. I think your odds are not good. In other words, I still do not believe the contest is fair. I like to win. If you accept then begin. This time, we will allow you to surprise us with your great abilities, if you can. My sneaks are ready. If you do not accept then we are finished."

Thiery examined the courtyard. There seemed to be three ways out: the portcullis, the iron bound door containing the three-inch peep, and six-feet above it, there hung a thick oaken barricade, topped with iron wheels set in long tracks. It reminded him of a large, sliding barn door, though reinforced to keep an enemy out, or possibly to keep something in. Suddenly it moved as the morning mist began to dissipate. The sneaks noticed it too. Some of them took a step back. Thiery wondered what Squilby meant by 'all is not as it seems.'

It wouldn't do to be taken by surprise again, and so his mind worked every angle.

The sneaks were nimble and wore light leather jerkins, but a dagger could not stop a blow from his quarterstaff. They would simply have to give way if he ran through their circle, swinging. His weapon was eight feet long, and their weapons less than a foot. They might all rush at once and overwhelm him, but as long as he kept moving he could strike sudden blows, and attack again from a safe distance.

Wondering from where some surprise might come, he looked again towards the tavern and the adjacent alley. Thiery saw the corner of a green hood, and still more disconcerting, the tip of white yew wood. He had been right. Whoever the fellow was, he carried a long bow. An archer then, and maybe he, or Pip for that matter, was part of the contest.

Settling on a plan, Thiery raised his arms toward heaven, allowing his staff to lightly scrape the barricade hanging above Squilby's door. The huge portal moved slightly in response.

The effect on the sneaks was instantaneous. Each held his dagger up, backing away, chests heaving.

Squilby roared at them from behind the door, "Hold your ground. What is going on?"

Dropping his arms, Thiery stepped in close to the peep-hole, "I agree to your terms, Master Squilby." Turning, he sprinted through the widening circle of boys, sweeping one sneak off his feet as he went.

Thiery heard Squilby screaming something unintelligible. Halfway to his destination, Thiery risked a glimpse behind him. At that moment something went terribly wrong. Some unseen force grabbed his legs and sent him skidding upon his knees and outstretched staff.

Lurching to his feet, he only tripped and fell again. Then he watched as the sneaks quickly surrounded him, wary of his staff, but grinning. Above their heads, they twirled bolas; three leather cords attached to smooth stones. Looking down he realized one was already twined tight about his ankles. Even if he had his dagger to cut himself free, this new threat was formidable. Without a blade, he would need both hands to untangle his legs, and then he knew they would fall upon him.

Thiery rolled to his left as one of the sneaks let loose with his weapon. The bola whirred past his head. Thiery struck out as he hopped up, jabbing the breath from one of his opponents. The sneak dropped his dagger, and fell back gasping.

The dagger was a few feet away, but then another bola wrapped itself around him. Theiry hopped forward awkwardly trying to keep his balance, even as two more bolas whirled about his neck and head—the stones struck blows to his chin, cheek, and temple in rapid succession. He fell to the ground stunned, wrapped tightly in a web of cords. His staff clattered, rolling from his fingers.

Thiery lay with the cold, hard cobbles pressed to his face, staring at the portcullis only thirty feet away, wondering if more blows would come, or if they would be satisfied with their victory. Suddenly thirsty, he closed his eyes and whispered to God as he waited. "They that wait upon the Lord shall renew their strength; they shall mount up with wings as eagles; they shall run, and not be weary; and they shall walk, and not faint."

He opened his eyes. Four sneaks stood close by, arguing whether or not to teach him more of a lesson. It seemed that their deliberations had ended in a tie. They looked towards Squilby's eye, but he kept silent. Then they turned to the sneak that Thiery had struck in the stomach, he still gasped for breath.

"What do you think Bard?" The biggest of the sneaks asked. "Does he deserve one more thrashing or shall we leave him be?"

The seconds passed slowly as Bard held his stomach, grimacing, an occasional noise squeaking from his lips. The chances of him choosing to let Thiery go didn't seem very good; he tensed, thinking of them striking blows while he lay so vulnerable, not even able to cover his face. Thiery looked past their legs and saw the man with the green hooded cloak, now completely visible near the alley. He was slender, yet bigger than the sneaks.

Raising his bow he nocked an arrow. It had a round wooden tip like the nose of a court jester. It was the kind of arrow used for mock battles during the fairs. A dozen more balanced in a line before the archer, tips on the ground and shafts raised vertical within easy reach.

The sneak, called Bard, finally spoke forth his answer. But though his lips moved, the sound was masked by grunts and cries of pain from his fellows. The green archer fired so fast and unerringly, that had they been metal tipped arrows, each boy would have been impaled twice before taking as many steps. As it was the missiles hit hard against backs, legs, and arms. Sneaks tumbled in all directions to escape another painful barrage.

Once again Squilby screamed in rage. Thiery rolled his body over once and grasped the dagger's hilt tight, sawing at his bonds. In seconds, he was free. He grabbed his staff and sprinted through the gate and into the street.

Thiery looked about with a broad grin, but the green archer was gone. Behind him, a rattling of chains caused him to jump, and the portcullis crashed closed. Squilby whistled and the Sneaks flocked to the three-inch peep. Their hushed consultation dragged on for minutes. Would Squilby require a rematch? Would he cry foul?

A moment later Pip stood beside Thiery, his face sullen. He gripped the portcullis and stared into the throng of sneaks across the courtyard; he looked worried, almost scared.

Thiery couldn't help but feel bad for him. "What's wrong?"

"Master Squilby will be angry with me." Still, he kept his gaze locked before him.

"What for?"

"I was supposed to … re … re … something or other?"

"Reconnoiter."

"Yeah, reconnoiter, and I'm pretty sure I didn't do it right."

"Why not?"

"Oh, it was that green fellow." Pip's shoulders slumped. "We call him the Green Archer, but everyone knows that he's really Diego Dandolo. Well, at least we're pretty sure. He's always one step ahead, making his presence felt among us, playing little tricks, sometimes foiling our interviews, like he did just now. He really makes Master Squilby mad, and if I had been able to stop him, or if I had unmasked him and made our suspicions certain, the Master would have been mighty pleased with me. I should have known the Green Archer wouldn't be taken so easy."

"I'm beholden to him for helping me out, whoever he is. But I am sorry for you." Thiery meant it, and his sincere concern for the sneak was obvious.

Pip turned and looked at him, allowing a lopsided grin, and a flurry of dimples.

"Thanks. I watched as he laid out his arrows, and so I began to creep behind him unnoticed. As he nocked the first arrow he said 'Watch where you step'. I froze, not knowing if he was speaking to me, but it seemed that he likely was. The next thing I knew my feet snapped together, bound by a rope. Then I was hurtling along the ground towards the tavern. I smashed into the side of the building, and then the rope pulled me up the wall and on to the roof. All the way up there. Boy did I ever mess up.

"By the time I climbed down, the Green Archer was gone, and you were standing here." Pip looked more closely at Thiery. His eyes widened. "I thought that was mostly dirt all over you, but you took a beatin'."

"It must look worse than it really is, though I must say that I've felt better. More than anything right now I'm thirsty, but I don't want to leave until I find out whether or not I passed Master Squilby's test."

Both boys looked into the courtyard at the sound of the metal peep cover scraping closed. The biggest sneak came running towards them. Pip whispered from the corner of his mouth. "That's Bully, he's got a mean streak."

Bully stopped a few feet from the portcullis with his arms folded across his chest. He looked like he was a few years older than Thiery, and everything about him portrayed arrogance. He had a handsome but cruel face. He was smiling while gritting his teeth.

"There's your endorsement." He threw something like a coin onto the cobbles near Thiery's feet. Bending to pick it up, Thiery saw that it was a square piece of tin with a flying dragon etched upon it. When he stood back up, Bully tossed Thiery's dagger through the gate spinning it violently. Thiery caught the hilt as if it had been gently handed over.

"Thanks." Thiery drew forth the knife he had taken from the fallen sneak. It was a much better weapon, and it fit his scabbard well.

"No. Squilby said you took it fairly. You keep both."

"Tell Bard that it was just a contest, and if he wants his dagger back then I will gladly give it."

Bully didn't answer, but turned slightly to address Pip's questioning look. "Squilby says you can come back in three days and no sooner."

Pip reeled as if struck by a physical blow. Then Bully added as he turned to walk away, "And your brother too."

Pip's face turned pale, and his eyes glistened with welling tears.

Distressed

Count Rosencross and the Priest watched it all from an alley near the Six Toed Tavern, completely hidden from onlookers. They could see much, but they could not hear anything beyond the screams of Squilby, and the sounds of the skirmish.

"You, see?"

"No, I don't see."

"It's the boy, Thiery, your son, and he lives," Rosencross whispered.

"No!" The Priest was sure of himself. "It is just a boy. Boys may look alike, but that is not my son. He is dead—sacrificed."

"Did you actually see that he was dead?" Rosencross persisted.

"Of course I did. I looked in upon him. He did not breathe. He couldn't have, for the amount of poison was prodigious."

Count Rosencross had never, ever heard anything like this before. The Priest's words were clear, but his voice seemed uncertain. Yes, the Priest had his doubts, though maybe he did not even know it himself; too prideful to acknowledge the possibility.

The Priest's grip on Rosencross had been more powerful than he cared to admit. Yet now its strength had lessened, ever so slightly. Rosencross stared at the Priest. The Priest averted his gaze; when had that ever happened?

"I haven't the time for this. And with the games starting tomorrow, neither do you."

Rosencross looked back to the closed portcullis where the boy and the sneak talked in hushed tones. The boy was dirty and bruised, but still the resemblance was strong.

What could it mean if the boy still lived? Something deep inside the Count hoped it was so, but something else in him feared the consequences of such a thing.

Before he heard the familiar yet irritating voice, Rosencross realized someone had come up alongside him. "Ah, Count, funny finding you here at this early hour." It was Diego Dandolo. "I thought I heard you speaking to someone."

There was that annoying grin and questioning tilt of the head.

Rosencross turned and placed his back to the nearby wall, looking, as naturally as possible, to the spot where the Priest had been standing just moments before. He was gone—withdrawn from their presence without a sign or sound.

The Count simply smiled in return.

"Oh … I'm familiar with that look," Diego began, "a more deprecating smile I've never seen. Do you dislike me that much?"

There, he had done it again. Somehow, Diego had put the Count on the defensive. How was he able to parry every blow, evade every assault, and drive home every thrust? Rosencross, thinking on Diego's methods, suddenly had an idea. "I hoped you wouldn't notice," Rosencross said, this time his smile was genuine. "But now that you have, I'll not try to hide my dislike of you in future."

Diego's eyes sparkled at this. A chuckle escaped from his lips, and his smile, also, seemed genuine. "The Chronicler and I are breakfasting in the tavern here, and he's sent me to invite you in. Would you care to join us?"

Rosencross did want to see the Chronicler again, but he also wanted to follow the boy. He hesitated, looking back toward the portcullis. The boy and the sneak had left the gatehouse and were now walking down Witchum Street. He made his decision to follow, but at the same time he preferred not to have his intention known.

Diego's eyes followed those of Rosencross. "Do you have some special interest in them, or are you here just to enjoy the show."

"The show?"

"Can it be that you aren't aware of what goes on here? I so enjoy it when I know something that another man does not." Diego's smile was warm but the words were taunting to a man like Rosencross. He would not get pulled in though.

"It's a big city," Rosencross began cautiously, "I'm an infrequent visitor. I'm sure there's a lot to learn."

"Interesting." Diego looked around the narrow alley, eyebrows raised, frowning, "You just happened to be here? In the dark, talking to …" He shrugged his shoulders and tilted his head again.

Rosencross narrowed his eyes and the heat came upon his face. "I like dark alleys. Anything could happen to anyone. They're dangerous, especially for a man like you."

"Let us not digress to angry words, Count, not you and I. I shall not pry into the matter further. Instead, let me offer a peace token between us. I only meant to say that I like to be of help to others. Knowledge is quite valuable, as you know. Shall I share with you then what it is that goes on here? No doubt you can find out from others, but I would be honored to be the one."

"As you like." Rosencross responded stiffly.

"Very gracious of you, Count. Let's see then. People don't eat at the Six Toed because of the food, not that it's terribly bad, but it's not good either. Yet the tavern is frequented by many of the citadel's masters or their representatives anyway. They come to see what Master Squilby is up to. He's gained notoriety for many things, one of which is his open policy." Diego paused.

"Which is?"

"He lets any boy from the street interview. Every once in a while one wins a recommendation, like today."

"But someone helped him; the man in green." Rosencross glanced away as he spoke. Now he could barely make out the boys. They were gathered with a growing crowd around a large wooden crate.

"So he did, but anything goes with Master Squilby. It won't be long and you'll become familiar with his ways." Diego said, and then he too caught sight of the gathering, and the crate, and a man climbing upon it.

"Ah, a town crier—it will be news of the games most likely. The whole city will be abuzz with the thrill of it. King Strongbow knows how to move the masses. A hundred or so of the criers scatter about the city repeating their tale scores of times. Look how the people materialize as if from nowhere. They hunger for it as much as they do for the games themselves.

"And that one there, he's one of the best ... no, we'll hear him fine from where we are, his voice carries well, and you'll see as he prepares to speak, the hush that follows. Now, I personally struggle with some of the poeticisms, while many in that crowd will take notes and go discuss it for hours, but I prefer the more straightforward tidings."

Just then, the great bells of the city, slowly, methodically, rang out to the tune of ten chimes. The light of dawn was chasing the coolness of the night away, and the remaining pockets of fog seemed first to run for the bog lands, but then having to pass through pockets of sun, they striated and wisped away to nothing.

The crier took a deep breath, and bellowed:

Have you not heard ...
They shout the sport of kings,
They praise the sport of kings,
Yet there are some who berate the sport of kings,
But I say, we play the sport of kings and the sport of his people
With, I say, with his people,
The sport of kings and the sport of his kingdom.
Will you join us then, people of the land, in sport?"

The crowd roared in response, cheering and raising their arms. The crier waited for them to quiet, nodding his head in approval at their robust retort. He continued with the clenching of his fist:

But what of the naysayers? Will you not climb aboard?
My city bells invite thee to the chase, the crossing swords,
The feats of strength most to be remarked,
This is the sport of kings ... but my people, it is for you.
Come see the glory, the image of war,
The image of war without the guilt,

My city bells, they ring, come up I say, you ugly beast,
Its roar puts fear into the belly,

its claws and teeth that rip and tear,
Tell me the man's a dragon hunter,
a giant slayer, a wielder of weapons,
And I your king love him at once.
Come up I say, you ugly beast,
Tell me the man's a hunter, and I love him at once.

The hunt is all that's worth living for
all time is lost what is not spent in its embrace
it is like the air we breathe
if we have it not we die.
It's the sport of kings, the image of war without the guilt,
And only five-and-twenty per cent its danger.

And, for the sport of kings,
we increase the number of the dead,
yet only five-and-twenty per cent. A bargain for the people.
We invite you to the chase, the games, the sport of kings.
But the death and the guilt,
They're only five-and-twenty per cent.
What say you, people? what say you of your bargain?

Again the crowd roared their assent—thirsting for the sport of kings. The crier turned his head back and forth, staring into the eyes of each spectator, waiting, waiting … waiting … and then a mouth from the crowd yelled, "What sport will we see?"

The crier grinned, smiled, and then chuckled as his head slowly tilted back. Suddenly tense, his stance widened, his arms extended, and the crowd hushed. "What sport indeed? Fist-to-cuffs, quarterstaff, swords, man versus man, beast versus beast, and man versus beast. Some games may seem ill equipped for fairness or equality of arms, but listen close, and watch with wisdom.

"The deficiency of strength may be greatly supplied by Art; but the want of Art will suffer heavy loss despite ones strength. Strength I say. And what does the word imply? Likely you've guessed it, for what greater strength can there be than giants. And three of the Anakims have just arrived. Glory, battle, and blood are their desire. Who will fight them? Man or beast, or both. Come and see."

The crier jumped from his platform, picked up the wooden box, and ran for his next oration. The crowd, after watching him go, was indeed immediately abuzz.

Diego Dandolo whistled low. "You see, Count, how the masses are corralled and coaxed to do the master's bidding."

He knew it was awkward to break away from their conversation now, but if he waited any longer the boys would be too far-gone. "I have some things to attend to. Please thank the Chronicler for his invitation, perhaps another time. Good day to you, Diego."

"And to you, Count."

He almost lost the boys, due to the large crowd that was discussing the coming games and the news of the town crier. But he caught sight of them turning onto Potshard and making their way towards Flummery Gate, one of the many portals between Old and New City.

Here they bought some food and drink from a street vendor, paid for by the boy, and then they sat down by a tiny child just outside the shadow of Flummery Gate. The youngster couldn't have been older than five or six—off and on he leaned his head against the sneak while carefully eating every morsel of his meal. The three talked and laughed for a quarter of an hour, while Count Rosencross watched intently from a trinket shop across the street. Soon, both older boys arose and departed their separate ways. The little child sat back down on a ragged cloth, coughed violently for a spell, and then held out a bowl, with his slight bone-protruding arms, to once again beg.

Rosencross reached into his purse as he passed the little beggar: he felt the cool flat coins, rubbed them against each other, and then withdrew his hand—empty. He chided himself for the weakness to which he had almost succumbed. And anyway, why waste money on a child who was sickly, and not likely to live many more years? Why delay the suffering of such a boy? That was the strange illogical tonic by which he soothed his objecting conscience. It bothered Rosencross greatly that he must even have these arguments with himself.

Thiery, if it was indeed him, was moving much faster now, and Count Rosencross had no time to ponder the strange flicker of emotion caused by the encounter with the weakling child of the street.

A Home of Sorts

"You look distressed, sir," Thiery said, "I am sorry. I should have asked you first, they just seemed so pitiful, and the words came out before I meant them to."

"No, no, it'll be fine, you've already apologized, and what harm can there be in giving dinner to some starving children?"

"A dinner party, not just dinner, but a party ..." Suzie looked back and forth between Gimcrack and Thiery. "Didn't you say we could have a dinner party? That would be more festive than just dinner. I mean we could sing, and tell stories, and all sorts of fun things ... like a game, oh a game, and we'd make sure that we tell them wonderful things about God. I won't complain if you want to change it back to dinner only though, I certainly wouldn't do that, Gimcrack, sir, oh how terrible that would be of me to complain, just terrible." Suzie looked at Gimcrack with her big eyes, clenching her tiny hands under her chin.

Gimcrack smiled down at her hopeful face. "Of course, we'll have a party, my dear."

"May I make a suggestion?" Suzie asked, only it sounded more like, "May I make a sugstenin."

Gimcrack laughed, and his often-downward spiraling disposition broke free from his familiar habit of worry; he patted Suzie's head. "I would love to hear your suggestions, for you're the only lady here, and it will need a lady's touch to make it a true party."

"That is just what I was thinking." Suzie beamed. "I could make this a real home of sorts, with a few things… " Here she paused.

Gimcrack didn't respond. He was staring out the window-slit that commanded a view of the grave-yard.

Thiery tried to help Suzie out. "A few things, huh …"

Still, Gimcrack stared away, seemingly lost in his thoughts.

"What few things, do you need, Suzie?" Thiery asked, raising his voice conspicuously.

"Oh, well, using only one candle at night like we've been doing is just fine for ourselves, but when we're having company, and a party besides, I was hoping that we might use five … six … or maybe even seven, and a lamp too. Does that sound like it would be okay? Because if it's too much we'll make do with whatever you think is wiser."

Gimcrack mumbled something to himself.

Thiery shrugged his shoulders. "What else do you need? Just tell us everything at once."

"Well, it sure would look pretty to have some flowers, I had a lot of flowers drying at Oded's stables—they make things feel nice. Now, I don't want to seem like I'm asking for too much, but since it is a party and not just dinner, there should be a little extra I think. Like cake, I bet those boys don't get cake much.

"And we could serve some apple cider, and some bread, and cheese, and even some meat, just a little anyway. And if there's any fruit in the market, that sure would be festive, it would look real pretty until we eat it. And some kind of vegetable, like sugar snaps, or carrots, or maybe a cuke. I bet those boys aren't very good about getting enough vegetables. What do you think, Gimcrack, sir?"

"Huh … oh vegetables, yes I like 'em good enough. Listen, why don't you two run out and get what we need. I have some thinking to do. There's a little market on Feudalfun, just a couple blocks from here, do you know where that is, Thiery?"

"Yes, sir, I saw it this morning; we should be back in half an hour."

"They're late," Gimcrack whispered, peering into the graveyard, wide eyed. "I can't believe we're out here in the dark again. And it's a bit too cold for me tonight."

"Sorry, sir, I just thought this was a good landmark to meet them by. I couldn't think of anything else. But I don't mind waiting by myself if you'd like to go in."

"As if I would leave you alone out here after what happened, and just last night. My mind's still all discomfibulerated from the whole terrifying mess."

"Yes, sir, I've noticed that you've been thinking a lot lately; I mean your thinking has taken on a noticeable aspect to it."

Gimcrack tilted his head, and caressed his chin in a real dandified thinking pose, like a statue that Thiery had once seen. "Well that's real good of you to notice, Thiery. You see I've got a mind that likes to be active about the mysteries of the how and the why of things. I suppose it's a gift that God, in His goodness, decided to give me. That's what good old Staffsmitten used to tell me.

"I suppose that's why I like to invent things. Anyway, I've been trying real hard to figure out the hows and whys of last night. There's something to know, I just know it deep down in my knower. But like I said, being discomfablastigated from the night's more petrifying—now that's the word for it—the night's more petrifying aspects, I'm not quite able to put the pieces together."

"It sure was scary." Thiery said.

"Scary! You have a way of understating a thing. But, don't be too hard on yourself, my boy; your vocabulary will grow as you get older. Until then you could always add words like really, really, really scary. You see how that works. But it's also in the way you say it, not just the words themselves. It didn't sound much like a scary night the way you said it. In fact, if the tale needs telling, and I'm around, you best let me do it, so I can give it the proper feel."

"I will, sir. And I'll pray that God clears your mind and gives you the knowing that you're looking for."

Just then Thiery thought he saw something move out of the corner of his eye—something in the grave-yard. Gimcrack must have seen it too, for he let out a deep breath and said, "Thank our God. They're here, and now we can get inside."

But Thiery was startled by the voice of Pip just behind him. He had come in from another street, and not used the grave-yard at all. Thiery must have been seeing things then.

"You must be Gimcrack, Sir, and I'm Pip. Pip at your service, and this here's my little brother Percival, his proper name is Pup, but that's no name for such a hero as him. Is it? He's quite brave, my brother is."

Percival was small; small might be too big a word for him. His legs and arms held up his tattered clothes like a shriveled dead man. Thiery once saw an uncovered burial mound in which the corpse lay with his armor, sword, and shield draped about him; things that no doubt fit when he was strong, young, and alive, but in the grave it made the dead man look even more emaciated and well … dead.

Percival's eyes were lively though, and they looked at Gimcrack, imploring.

"Percival the brave seems very fitting for such a boy." Gimcrack said, smiling at the little one.

Pip nudged Percival. Percival squeaked, "Thank you, sir." Then he looked back at Pip as if to see how he'd done. Pip winked. Percival smiled, and life and joy spread across his little face. Then a shiver almost knocked him down. "Oh, It's cold, Pip."

"And he's unerringly precise and to the point. I'm cold too." Gimcrack rubbed his hands furiously together. "Let's go and have ourselves a dinner party. I always say one dinner party in the pot is worth ten sandwiches in the ... pantry ... or something like that."

Pip raised himself up, taut, and ready to spring, "Oh, don't tell me, sir, I'll figure that one out ... never heard that one ... um ... having trouble with the whole dinner party inside a pot compared to a pile of sandwiches ... yet ... oh it sure sounds like a good un, but I'll have to give up. Could you tell me what the saying means, sir? Just in case I hear that one again, then I'll be ready. I'm an eager one to learn things."

"Okay, let's see." Gimcrack looked alarmed. He began to speak under his breath as they walked, "A dinner party in a pot and sandwiches in a pantry, ten to one, one to ten ... doesn't seem to make a lot of sense ..." His panicky lip curling showed signs of emerging.

Thiery leapt in. "I suppose many of those sayings are more of something fun to say than to understand what they mean."

"Exactly right!" Gimcrack's panicky lip retreated. "They add spice and mystery to life, and this here dinner party in a pot saying, is one of the best for that kind of thing."

They opened the secret door. Horatio's hulking form met them at the bottom of the tower. His cold nose pressed against Percival and Pip, sniffing enthusiastically.

Percival giggled and, without a shred of fear, wrapped his arms around the wolf's neck. "I love you big doggy."

Dinner Party

Horatio instinctively stayed close to the little boy, protecting him, helping him along the uncertain climb.

As they made their way carefully up the creaking stairs, winding along the tower's perimeter, they could see a warm glow at the top, and hear the soft pattering of feet and a sweet humming that hit high beautiful notes of praise.

Slowly they left the dark and cold behind them, moving ever closer to the increasing warmth and light.

One of the stairs creaked louder than the rest. The humming stopped; the pitter of feet paused, but the creaking stairs continued. Soon they were in view of the landing, and Suzie's wide eyes and open mouth could be seen peeking around a post.

Suddenly her eyes twinkled in recognition, her smile swum into dimples, and her hands clapped noiselessly as she disappeared back into the chamber.

Tiny Percival's voice squeaked along with the stairs, "I like her."

On the landing, the party of boys and dwarf stared into the fire-lit room—only there wasn't a fire—Thiery had always thought that the sight of a fire warmed a person's heart and made a room feel jolly, more than most anything could. Yet this room, prepared by loving little hands, twinkling with seven candles and a lamp, adorned with flowers and cloth spread upon the table, and rumbling their tummies with red and green apples, bread, meat, cheese, cider, and even cake, was the most fire-lit room Thiery had ever seen.

Suzie stood by the table and curtsied.

The boys bowed.

Everyone looked about, unsure of what to do next. Everyone but Gimcrack. It was exciting for Thiery to see Gimcrack take charge in such a way; after all, he was their elder. And how uncomfortable it often was, to know that Thiery, and even one as young as Suzie, knew more about God, His word, His precepts, His ways, than the adult whom they now dwelled with.

Thiery and Suzie had been praying for him, asking God to make him one whom they could trust with their souls. For who knew, perhaps God intended Gimcrack to be as a father to them, maybe even become their father. They prayed, and they watched with an eye towards thanksgiving.

Then, there was always Oded. He was guardian to both Thiery and Suzie; if only they knew where to look for him. He was big and strong, and kind, and he had a simple, unquestioning faith; he loved to remember and tell of God's goodness in his life. But, even though they were yet children, they understood that Oded was not quite like others. Still, who knew, perhaps God intended Oded to be their father. After all, Oded's faith had become Thiery's faith, and Thiery would ever be thankful for him. He would ever hold him in the highest esteem. He would honor him, and for that matter, he would honor Gimcrack also; they were two imperfect men, but they were the men that God saw fit to pour grace and love into Thiery's and Suzie's lives. He would honor them, and in so doing he would honor God.

Gimcrack walked into the warm chamber, and stepped alongside Suzie. "Pip, Percival, I welcome you to our ... well as Suzie puts it, to our home of sorts. And I pray that the God of Noah would bless you both, that He would draw you to Him as He has drawn me, and that your hearts would be humble before Him always. I pray that you would both seek His truth, and beware the lies of the false gods all around us. I pray that Thiery, Suzie, and I would be your servants this night.

"All right then you young gentlemen, come and meet your hostess."

Pip came forward, his shoulders back, with Percival just behind, gripping his brother's pant leg. "Pip, at your service. It would be my important pleasin' to always be ready to help you in any way you could muster."

Percival chimed in, "Me too." And then he looked at Pip to see how he had done. Pip winked. Percival smiled.

"And," Pip continued, "we thank you very nicely for invitin' us to this really nice dinner party. We've never been invited to any such thing before. And we're giantly pleased to see all these niceties on our behalf. Aren't we Percival?"

"Yep. Giants?"

"Once, we watched through a big window; it was a dinner party with fine ladies and men, children, and good food, and such. I told Percival then, that we ought never to look in a window like that again, cause we weren't likely to ever experience such things. You see, it put an ache in our hearts. And now look at all this. This is loads better than that other party, this is really fine. Isn't this fine Percival?"

His head bobbed. "Better than fine. It's better. I like you, Suzie."

Suzie giggled. "I like you too, Percival."

Pip patted his little brother on the shoulder. "Percival, he's got a way with words. I have hopes that he could be one of them town criers or even a bard. Still a little hard to tell how his singing voice might turn out. But, for bein' five it sounds good to me. High hopes is what I've got for him. He's a pretty good beggar, but he doesn't seem to be doing too well with the cold weather, getting sick and stuff, and anyway he doesn't get to keep any of his beggin's."

"This is the best home ever." Percival's attention had turned to the smells and sights upon the table, "Is that cake?" He pulled on Pip's leg and pointed at the round, frosting covered delight.

The rest of the small party was drawn in; again someone's tummy rumbled. Gimcrack blessed the food. They ate, savoring the simple fare; and the two guests, while slightly embarrassed, truly enjoyed the sincere attention of their hosts. They played games, sang songs, recited a passage from Job, and talked as if they'd been friends for a very long time. They all agreed that it must have been the best dinner party that ever was.

Later, Thiery showed them how well trained Horatio was. They clapped and cheered at Horatio's tricks.

"He is quite smart, and obedient," Thiery began, "I've not been training animals very long, but I still think it extra ordinary that he learns so fast, especially since he was wild when I found him. A puppy yes, but as you can see, he's more grown than puppy."

Gimcrack suddenly sat upright, his face strangely troubled. "I'd forgotten that … you found him … oh no, oh no, it cannot be, but now it makes sense. Oh, my poor friend."

"What?" Thiery was so alarmed that he forgot to say sir.

"Don't you see, my boy? Think about where you found Horatio? It was not just a cave, but also someone's home. Mine and Staffsmitten's."

"I don't understand, sir?"

"I had been gone a very long time, so I would not have known of him, but Staffsmitten was always collecting and studying God's creatures. He was even writing a book about it, a bestiary."

"I see. You think Horatio was Staffsmitten's wolf, and that's why he's so tame."

"He must have been, at least to a great degree, I'm sure of it now. Why else would Horatio go berserk and start digging in the grave-yard?"

"Grave-yard, sir?" And then he too understood. It made perfect sense for Horatio to dig up a grave, if that grave held a living man, and that man was his master.

"He called my name," Gimcrack cried. "It was mumbled, but it was my name. He was calling me to help him, and I let him down. Oh, I let him down. And now those inky-stinky rotten apple splatted Dragon Priests have got him. How could I let him down like that?"

"But, sir, you couldn't know. It was dark, and he wasn't talking right. We thought he was trying to get us, to do us harm. But just think, he's most likely alive. We have hope, sir. With God's help, we can find Staffsmitten yet."

"I suppose, but in this great big city, how can we possibly find him now? If only I hadn't been so afraid I surely would have known him, even in the dark."

"Sir, what were the chances of you and I finding him the first time, buried beneath the earth, in this great big city, and we weren't even looking for him. I say, no chance at all, but with God all things are possible."

"Yes, that is the way to look at it; I'll try not to berate myself over my dismal failure any more, but instead, I'll press on, trusting to Him who knows all—" Gimcrack's mouth dropped open, he grabbed his hair with both hands, and then he smacked his forehead. "By all the flabby aghasteriferous things, my eyes have just been opened again! Thiery, my boy, there were two empty graves, and who was it that supposedly died fighting alongside Staffsmitten?"

Thiery looked over at Suzie as he began to understand. Suzie was leaning into the conversation—as were Pip and Percival—trying unsuccessfully to figure out what the second empty grave signified.

"Just maybe," Gimcrack said, answering his own question, "Lord McDougal was in that other grave—and maybe he too is alive!" Gimcrack's grin erased all signs of his previous distress.

"I knew it, I knew it." Suzie's face filled with joy. "Isn't God good to me, we'll find him, and rescue him, and then … oh, I can hardly wait."

"Hold on little sweetie," Gimcrack said, "We don't know anything for sure. There are a lot of ifs here. We'll simply pray for wisdom, put it all in God's hands, and do our best to follow wherever He might lead us. Duty bids us find our friends, but we've some formidable challenges ahead of us."

Gimcrack began pacing, circling the table. "First, Staffsmitten must have been drugged, otherwise why would he have acted so strangely?

"Hmm, an apothecary. Then there's an army of freaky priesties who sneak about in the dark, and a troublesome matter of not even knowing where they are, or where to start. I won't even begin thinking about what to do if we do find them or I'll just depress myself into feeble inaction."

"Yes, Gimcrack, sir." Suzie couldn't stop clapping and wiggling in her seat. "I have an idea where to start, oh, oh, Thiery said just today that the Citadel has a puffy hairy."

"A puffy hairy?" Gimcrack looked at Thiery, who shrugged.

Suzie looked surprised and a little confused. "You know. You just said that was how they drugged our friends."

Gimcrack smiled, "Exactly right, apothecary is how you pronounce it, but I do like the sound of a puffy hairy."

"Me too." Percival giggled, but it quickly digressed into a cough. By the time he finished, his skin was white; there was a blue tinge around his lips, and Pip had to steady him in his chair. After a few minutes of labored breathing, Percival looked at everyone through red rimmed eyes; eyes that were a little glassy with a far away aspect to them. "I'm okay."

Pip pushed his chair back and stood up. "I've got something to say if I could. Percival and I ... well ... you see, no one has ever treated us the way you all have. And it's about the most mighty fine thing we've ever had. We don't have many things like what a person could own or have stolen from him. But this mighty fine thing you've given us ... well ... no one can ever take it away.

"I just wanted to say thank you for it, and hearing how faithful you are to these friends that you thought were dead, well it makes a person think. We'd like to be your friends

and you can know that you've always got a friend in us ...
Pip at your service, always at your service."

"Me too."

The Chronicler's Ship

F ergus had been without McDougal for two days, and it was now the morning of the third—the day of the games. The games at which McDougal would have shown all of Hradcanny and the kingdom's subservient lords, and lesser kings, that he was still a warrior to be reckoned with; yes he was without his lands, without his family, but he would have shown them. If only McDougal had let Fergus come with him, to be by his side at the battle where he had fallen.

There was a terrible ache within him. As shield-bearer, it was only right that he should have been with him. He had always been there in the past, ever since McDougal's father had given him the charge. Not to be there the day he had fallen—it was so pointed, so piercing, so contrary to all that he had ever imagined, that he struggled against the temptation to question his God, to ask why. While the temptation was there, he still chose to thank God for all that He had given him, to thank Him that he would one day see McDougal again. Fergus knew that believing and trusting in God was the most important thing, and he knew that McDougal had done just that.

Despite his sadness, McDougal had given Fergus a parting gift—a duty to fulfill following his lord's final command—protect the Lady Mercy. In fact he would not leave her side. When she went to her cabin, Fergus stood watch outside her door. And when she passed the doors threshold, he knew by her look, her smile, and her tender words, that she was grateful, not only that he was there, but that it was Lord McDougal who had put him there. It was such a noble calling; he praised God continually for this gift that tempered the hurting of his soul.

He also felt a special calling to protect Igi Forkbeard. Now that might have seemed strange to many, seeing that Igi was a powerful warrior much bigger and stronger than Fergus, but McDougal had seen fit to pursue this man's soul and one of the last things he had done was save Igi's life. Fergus would try and do the same. But he wasn't prepared for what came next.

They'd built a temporary shelter around Igi. Mercy was having a great deal of trouble keeping him in his sick bed. The sailors and Tostig's warriors found the interchanges quite amusing; in fact, Igi's complaining and Mercy's chastising were on display at the moment. Sir Tostig and Fergus stood a dozen paces away, looking across the harbor toward Old City, waiting and hoping that the Chronicler would send word of what they should do next. Every morning someone had come, and so they watched the wharf, and the people moving about it.

"Excuse me, sir." It was one of Tostig's men. "I brought Lady Mercy some things she requested, and I got a good look at the wounded man."

"Yes."

"Well, sir. It's that slaver that brought us down in the boats. The one who challenged God to free us … just before the dragon attacked."

Sir Tostig stiffened, his voice was harsh. "Are you sure?"

"I am, sir. I thought I recognized him yesterday, just by the sound of his voice. When I saw him sitting up just now, I knew for sure."

Tostig kept his eyes upon the wharf. Except for his white knuckles and clenched fist, one would think he'd left the discussion and forgotten to dismiss his man. Fergus had known little of Sir Tostig; that he was proud, as most princes of the kingdom were, that he was an able swordsman, a respected commander, and one who feared God. While on ship, there had been no one of equal rank for him to pass the time, and so Fergus was surprised to find that Sir Tostig often sought out his company, his conversation, and even his advice.

"Blagger." Sir Tostig's voice was stiff, but there was some other quality to it. Could it be that he was sad?

"Yes, sir."

"Let Lady Mercy know that I am requesting an audience on the forecastle deck, at her convenience."

"Yes, sir."

"Oh, and Blagger, do the men know what you've told me?"

"I don't think so, sir, not from my lips anyway."

"Very good, come join us after you've seen the lady."

"Yes, sir."

Fergus was encouraged to see that Tostig was at least outwardly calm. He knew a battle raged within him.

"Will you accompany me Fergus? I'd like to know a few things before Mercy comes."

"Gladly, sir." And so they walked slowly to the forecastle deck. Sailors gave them a wide berth, allowing as much privacy as could be expected on a ship with three-score men vying for space in the cool morning air.

"I've a mind to run him through." Tostig turned and looked Fergus straight in the eyes. Fergus didn't answer.

"I've never liked slaving, and now that I've been humiliated by it, even for such a short time, I've got a strong inclination to make sure he never does it again." By Tostig's expression and the tilt of his head, Fergus knew an answer was required, but he also knew that directly opposing a proud man's position could easily entrench that position within his breast.

"Will you wait till he's fully healed, sir, or would it be better just to get it over with?"

Sir Tostig's stare intensified, his brow furrowed, and then all at once he smiled. "Fergus, you know very well that I haven't decided on a course of action. I'm asking for your opinion, man. He enslaved a lord of the realm; and what of my men, shall I look the weakling before my own men when they find out he's here in our hands?"

"I'm sorry, sir. If it's my opinion you would like then I'd be happy to give it to you." Fergus retold the tale of how they saved Igi Forkbeard from the giants, his torture, his fear of the false gods, and how when McDougal stood against the Bachus priests, Igi, despite the odds and his own superstitions, stood by McDougal, and joined their small band. "And I can see him watching, and thinking about what we say and do, especially when we speak of God. Lord McDougal saw fit to risk his life for him twice, and so I'm inclined to ask for his pardon.

"Beyond that, by what you've said yourself, it was more the fault of Count Rosencross that you found yourself in danger of slavery, than it was the fault of Igi. While man-stealing is against the laws, slavery is not; your own people have many slaves. Was it even in Igi's power to free you? Or as far as he could tell, is it not likely that he believed it his duty to do just as he did? Admittedly, there is a great offense to be considered, and you will know better than I how to proceed in dealing with it."

Just then, Blagger announced the arrival of Lady Mercy. She came up the ship's ladder to the forecastle deck, and graced Fergus and Tostig with a playful curtsy and then an embarrassed scrunching of her nose—for the men looked overly serious.

"Lady Mercy, thank you for granting me this audience. It has just come to my attention who it is that you are taking care of. Could you please convey to me, to the best of your ability, what kind of character you believe your patient to have."

"I will." The warmth left Mercy's eyes. She continued carefully, for it was apparent to all that one of the lord's of the kingdom had just convened his court. "His manners are a little rough, but I don't know if that is as much a character flaw, as it is a lack of proper training in such things. He seems to me a very loyal soldier, and he blames himself for what happened to Lord McDougal. He has asked me many questions about God, especially concerning God's forgiveness. I believe he feels acutely the sins of his past, whatever they are, which, as you know, is a good and necessary place to be before one can repent and receive God's grace. Do you not agree, my Lord?"

"Yes, of course." Tostig paced the deck. "There are the laws of God, which only He can forgive the transgressions of, and then there are the laws of men, for which God gives man the power to mete out justice."

"Cannot man forgive also?" Mercy pleaded.

"Yes, but a mockery cannot be made of a society's laws or worse will men do."

"Cannot at least a punishment be lessened, especially in light of honorable and dutiful services rendered? Would you undo what Lord McDougal, your friend, has done? For your friend saw fit to rescue this man from certain death. My father was the king's brother. I am the king's niece, but because I follow the one true God, it is evident that my life is not worth much to the powers of this kingdom. We followers of God are in earthly danger, but not eternal danger, yet it is a great comfort that God has given me two capable fighting men to protect me on this earth. I know that Fergus will always be true, and I hope the same of Igi Forkbeard."

"Has Igi sworn himself into your service then?"

"Not that I have heard from his lips, but I have no doubt that he has, just the same."

"Is he well enough to dress and walk about?"

"He is healing well. I hoped he would stay fairly still for another day or two. If he exerts himself, some of his wounds will open. But, yes, I'm afraid he will be very happy to walk about."

"I have heard enough, then. Thank you, Lady Mercy. Blagger, see to it that Igi is dressed and armed. Then call our men to gather outside his quarters. I should like this to be done quickly."

The Verdict

Sir Tostig stood with his thirteen men: valiant, hand-picked, battle-tested, and strong. They were an imposing company, even striking, with their new armor and weapons supplied by the Chronicler—they shone.

Igi Forkbeard stood before them, his face bruised and cut, his clothes stained, his armor rent and battered, the hilt of his two-handed sword impressed with age and wear. Yet his large body, stout chin, and streaks of graying hair, mixed with the dignified bearing of a warrior who knew his skill, was something of equal beauty.

Fergus thought that there was something different about this Igi Forkbeard and the one they had found only four days before, but he couldn't figure exactly what it was.

"Igi Forkbeard. Do you know why you've been called before me, as lord and judge, this day?"

"I have an idea."

"Are you the Igi Forkbeard sung about in the ballad of the Quaking Wood?"

"I am." There was a slight stirring of approval from the fighting men and sailors.

"Are you the Igi Forkbeard, who is in the employ of Count Rosencross, as his slaver?"

"I was, but am no longer."

"You are no longer his slaver or you are no longer in his service at all?"

"He was unhappy that you and your men escaped, and that all my men perished. He no longer cared to keep me."

The color rose in Tostig's face. "The charge is man-stealing. Worse, the crime was enacted upon a lord of the realm. It's a crime worthy of death. What is your defense?"

Igi looked at the faces around him, spreading his stance slightly, resting his hand upon his sword. He stopped when he saw Lady Mercy and Fergus. He seemed to relax. "My defense is poor. For five years I've traded in men's lives. I've never lifted a hand against woman or child, but I've done things that I deserve death for, so I'll not deny your judgment.

"Count Rosencross is a secretive man, and I'm not one he shares his secrets with. I simply fought when fighting was to be done, and delivered, purchased, and sold slaves when they were put into my keeping. The part that pricks my insides is that I broke them when they needed breaking. Whether or not I live beyond this day, I'm done with slaving, and I've purposed my heart toward right things. I can't say how well I shall do at it. But that's the course I've set.

"As far as you and your men go, I believe I was acting as a slaver, and turning a blind eye to the details of it all. Not that I knew much, but I did know that you were a prince of the land, and that you were likely taken by underhanded means. I chose to believe that none of that was any of my business."

Tostig continued his inquiry, "Hmm. A boy and a white wolf came down that night and spoke to you on behalf of my company and me. We heard the battle between you and the dragon as we rowed away. You say all your men perished. What happened to the boy and how did you alone live?"

"As me and my men were being slaughtered by that beast, the boy drew back to the hill and fired his arrows. I was pressed into the earth; the dragon opened its great mouth to crunch my bones or swallow me whole, whichever it pleased. But it paused. I cried out; to your God I called, and in that instant an arrow pierced the creature's tongue.

"It let me go, and I rolled away, and as I tried to rise, it pinned me to the earth yet again. One of its claws pierced my armor and drew blood, but no more than that. Again the dragon paused, and peered into my eyes. And again I cried out to your God, and again one of the boy's arrows was sent straight and true. The arrow pierced the dragon's eye, sinking deep. It writhed and smashed; its tail like a falling tree crushed my men; its claws ripped and shredded. On all sides these beastly weapons flew about me, yet none struck me—only my men. They were all killed. And then the creature was gone, roaring through the wood.

"I stayed with the boy for two days. He fed me, and told me more about the God of Noah. Then he angered me, and so I left him. But first I gave him of my men's gold, armor, and weapons, and some information to keep him safe from future harm. I should not have left him, after what he did, but what's done is done. I owe him for my life, and I hope I get … rather that God gives me a chance to repay the boy."

Now Fergus could see what was different. Igi's idol that hung about his neck was gone, and the one upon his sword's pommel was gone too. Had Igi turned to God then?

"I, too, owe a debt of honor to that brave lad," Sir Tostig said. "Who is he? And what was the information you gave him?"

"His name is Thiery. He was training under Oded the Bear to be a ranger. He was told that Oded had been sick, likely dead. But Oded was never sick, only sent away on some excuse. The boy was given a sick tent to die in. I thought it likely that the boy had been sacrificed to the Dragon Priest's gods, only the sacrifice hadn't worked. I told him not to go back to Count Rosencross or he wouldn't live long, and that was all."

Fergus now made sense of the dead ants. So, they had been very close to finding Thiery; he could hardly wait to find Suzie and Oded and let them know. And now, one more of Lord McDougal's noble quests was open before him, and it would be Fergus's responsibility to find the boy, if he could.

"I find you guilty, Igi Forkbeard." Sir Tostig raised his clenched fist into the air. "Do you have anything to say before I decree your punishment?"

"No, Lord Tostig, your judgment is fair."

"I hereby press you into five years service. It shall begin immediately. After five years you are once again set free. Lady Mercy has need of personal guards and she has spoken on your behalf. Do you accept her as your lady, to serve and die for if necessary? I add to your sentence, that if you shall dishonor your post, then you become a dragon's-head, from which time anyone in the realm can hunt you down, and kill you, to be rewarded by the kingdom, as if you were a dragon yourself."

Igi knelt stiffly, and still his head was higher than Tostig's. "Thank you, Lord, you are gracious to me. I will honor my post, and lay down my life for the Lady Mercy."

So it was that Tostig gave Igi Forkbeard a noble purpose and a position of high standing, yet he cloaked the language and the meaning in terms that befitted punishment—Igi was made a slave. But it was clear that Igi did not see it as something to be ashamed of. With a tear in his eye, he knelt again, this time before Mercy.

Fergus felt an even greater respect for Tostig now. Somehow he had managed a great many things, quickly, and deftly. He had set aside his own pride and thoughts of vengeance for the betterment of others; he had softened the blow of Lord McDougal's terrible death instead of adding to its weightiness; he had sentenced a man to meaningful life instead of death, yet still keeping to the law; he had even elevated himself in the eyes of his men, who looked on approvingly; and he had added a great deal of protection to Lady Mercy. Yes, Lord Tostig was a wise man.

Fergus Unsure

"Skiff coming in!" The hail came from a sailor high up in the rigging. Sure enough, a boat was coming, but how he knew so soon which ship it was heading for was a mystery to Fergus. The harbor was bustling with activity. Ships from lords of the realm, merchant ships, the king's fleet, and numerous ships from other lands filled the river. Various small boats ferried men and women back and forth. It seemed that all the world was here for the games.

Igi was forced back to his quarters, for the loss of blood had made him dizzy; not that he would admit it. So when Mercy told him to go he went without complaint.

With one hand on the ship's ladder and another holding a cloth-covered object, a messenger from the Chronicler peered over the rail. Something white and gooey fell to the ship's deck as the object was passed to a sailor. There sounded from within what Fergus could only decipher as a fluttering of wings.

The messenger approached Lord Tostig, bowed, and handed him a sealed envelope. Everyone on board was making an effort to hear the news, yet everyone affected to be doing something else, anything. They hovered in their work like a flock of seagulls over a fishy morsel, not wanting to leave the vicinity.

Tostig didn't notice anything unusual, though, for he was more eager than anyone to get off the ship. He practically ripped the envelope from the messenger's outstretched hand. Fergus cleared his throat. He couldn't help himself; he had years of practice at subtly informing Lord McDougal when he wasn't behaving up to lord-like standards, and so the noise just naturally issued forth when he saw Tostig more eager than appropriate.

Lord Tostig paused, looked askance at Fergus, and raised his eyebrows slightly. Fergus raised his own eyebrows in return. There was a hint of a smile upon Tostig's lips, and then, more nobly, he removed the letter, unfolded it, turned it right side up, and began to read. From where Fergus stood, he could see that Tostig's spirit was still wound up, for his eyes ravaged the page. Then he read it again, more slowly this time. He handed the letter to Fergus.

"Finally!" Tostig exclaimed. "I don't think I would have done well bottled up here yet another day."

Fergus, always calm, read the letter slowly the first time through:

Send Lady Mercy, Fergus Leatherhead, and one of your men to me by noon at the Citadel, east portal. Someone will be there to let them in. Yet if they can be hurried along, they can travel with my messenger. Throughout the morning, your band can make its way to the arena in groups of two or three. Opening ceremony begins at two. Sit amongst the lower seats, spread out, but keep where your men can see you. I don't expect anything to happen the first day of the games, or perhaps at all, but we should be ready. The weather is cool enough that hooded cloaks will not seem unusual—at least for you and the Lady.

He looked up to see Lord Tostig grinning like a boy. "Well, Fergus, what do you make of that? I knew he'd want us there."

"Yes, sir, it will be pleasant to leave the ship."

But Tostig wasn't listening anymore; he was calling his men, and making plans for the day.

Blagger spoke to no one in particular, "That Forkbeard was none too happy to be left behind." The Chronicler's messenger sat next to him in the bow of the skiff; he showed no inclination to speak. The rowers bent their backs and pulled them toward the docks.

Mercy and Fergus sat in the stern. Mercy touched Fergus's arm. "Thank you, Fergus."

"Yes, my Lady."

"Do you know," Mercy said, sighing, "when my mother first got sick, I was so afraid that she would die, and then she did. Then the sickness got father and my brothers, and I not only began to fear for their lives, but I began to wonder what would happen to me—and then I felt as if I could never be safe. When they too died, as you know, my uncle was made my protector and guardian. The High King ...

"What could be more safe than that? And yet he gave me up, blinded by the philosophies of this world, to a cult that worships demons. But then I felt hope again when I saw Lord McDougal and you at the Seven Talons. My hope was well founded. God had sent my hero to rescue me. He had been my hero since I was a little girl. And when his family met with death and tragedy over and over, I prayed the more for him—that he would stand strong for God, wavering not in his faith, the truest kind of hero. And though I did not see him for a long time, he was very dear to my heart. But now, he too has died.

"Who can know what this day holds, or any other. But God has given me a very noble shield-bearer and an ex-slaver to protect me from this world's evils. So, how do you think I should exercise my faith now that I can rest in your protection? Which, by the way, I see to be just as trustworthy as Lord McDougal's was, for you are a paladin, Fergus, just as he was; a paragon of chivalry."

Fergus was stunned by the comparison. "My Lady, I cannot possibly equivocate myself with the qualities of Lord

McDougal. Please cease to compare me. I shall be happy indeed if, when I die, the words 'He was loyal and true' shall be written upon my marker." Fergus stiffened, for even mentioning those noble qualities scared him. Every day he prayed that God would help him to be just that. But he was afraid that he would fail in them.

The third quality to which he aspired was even too fearful a thing to mention—bravery. What if he should be found a coward? He shuddered.

"And as for your question of exercising your own faith, I think your question is no question at all. I think, instead, that you are about to tell me."

Mercy laughed. "Fergus Leatherhead, you won't even play the game. Tell me then, how did McDougal deal with your eccentricity?"

Fergus could not help but laugh at that, for no person he had ever known was more eccentric than McDougal, yet instead, Mercy had called Fergus the eccentric one. And he knew of course that he was not eccentric in the least. "I suppose he either ignored it or didn't realize it."

"He ignored it then."

"I thought we were talking about your faith, my Lady."

"Yes, well, in a roundabout way I was trying to tell you that it is in God that I shall place my trust and not in you or Igi. Please don't look offended. Would you have me put more trust in you than our God? You see, how could it have been any other thing, than God Himself, who brought you and Lord McDougal at the moment I was going to be killed? I praised Him in it to be sure, but very quickly all my attention was on man instead of God. So therefore, while I do believe that you are the means of God's protection, I am coming to realize that the means is unimportant, really, if God is not all-important in my heart."

"I think," Fergus mused, "that it was easier to discuss things with Lord McDougal than it is with you, my Lady."

"Well, at least, would you please call me Mercy instead of my Lady?"

"Of course, Lady Mercy."

Mercy shrugged her shoulders. "I agree with you there at least."

"Where, Lady Mercy?"

"That it was easier to discuss things with Lord McDougal."

Fergus decided it was time to talk about something else. "If you don't mind me saying, you've forgotten your hood, my Lady."

Mercy pulled her hood up. Only a close inspection could give an inkling of who hid beneath.

"I'll put it on since you and the Chronicler think it necessary, but do you really think anyone could recognize me in this sea of faces?"

There were more people squeezed into the streets than Fergus had ever seen. And as they climbed onto the dock, he felt a sickening doubt about purposely bringing Mercy into those swarming masses. He even thought he saw a somewhat familiar face peer, turn, and run away. He dismissed it, though, not recognizing anyone in that face. But the uneasy feeling it brought lingered.

And so, disembarked from their little craft, with the messenger and Blagger placed in the rear, Fergus began pushing his way through the excited throng. Mercy nestled safely between them all.

It would have been difficult for one person to make very good time, but with the four of them trying to keep together, it was almost impossible. The crammed bodies, pushing and bumping, were a pick-pocketer's paradise. A number of times, fingers from unseen bodies pulled at Fergus and the others, looking for coppers and unprotected pouches.

One jostling of the crowd was so severe that Fergus decided it was time for a rest. He turned his little crew, steering for the nearest open door.

It seemed they had tumbled into a curiosity shop. The storekeeper eyed them, appraising them in a matter of seconds. There was just enough space between displays for his corpulent middle to maneuver. His rounded girth quickly tapered at both ends; spiraling down were two twigly stocking-clad legs, with a small head resting upon the whole ungainly structure and two spidery arms suspended in the air, reaching. His fingers crawled lovingly across the merchandise as he approached. He somehow managed an unbelievably deep bow, marred only by a slight grunt as he righted himself.

"Welcome, welcome, yes, okay, welcome, oh, oh, oh, I can't believe it. Three days, three days, oh you've made me so happy, just so happy. Oh, and where have my manners been? I am Grimesby, and this is the shop of many lands and places and things from different ... lands and places. I will give you a bargain that you cannot refuse, cannot refuse. You see, I've had no customers for two days, at least none who have purchased anything, and so you can see what a position that puts me in. I shall have to practically give things away .... Uh, name your price; you've got me just where you want me. Bear in mind that I must eat, yes, I must eat."

Never having encountered such a strange spectacle, Fergus was at first completely taken aback, and so he said nothing.

Grimesby grabbed his round tummy and squeezed. "Have compassion, man, I am withering away ... must have more food."

This further redoubling of Grimesby's antics yet again caused Fergus some anxiety. He stalled with a non committal "hmm," overlapped with a sophisticated grunt—at least that is how he hoped it sounded. He simply had no idea what to say to this apparent madcap, and he had no idea how to extricate himself from Grimesby's presence with any semblance of dignity; for it would look foolish bouncing around from store to store, running from pick-pockets and strange store-keepers. Some protector he was turning out to be.

There was also the chance, although slight, that the man really was sane. Turning about and leaving, without any reasonable excuse was so obviously rude and beneath the station of Lady Mercy that Fergus could only grunt yet again, "Hmm."

Mercy kept her hood on, but stepped from behind Fergus. "Is that you, Mr. Gettlefinger?" she asked.

His hands dropped from his belly, his shoulders slumped, he gasped, and most transformative of all was his countenance—now crestfallen and shocked.

Mercy continued, "Why whatever is the matter, dear sir?"

"You have unmasked me." Gettlefinger withered. "I am undone." His voice changed completely; he now looked less fat, less spiderlike, and much less strange. Fergus found it fascinating that he could look so different, yet change not even a fragment of his costume.

Gettlefinger looked up, desperate. "Don't you see? I've fooled friends, co-thespians, and my own mother. I was a genius of the theatre ... I knew it was coming, the pressure was too great. Though it drives the knife ever so much deeper into my breast, I must hear from your own lips, you master of keen observation ... you lady of unparalleled perception, what was it that gave me away? What slip of my craft? I dare say I can handle it. Lay it before me, I beg you."

"Perhaps it will soften the blow then," Mercy answered, "to know that I have seen you on many occasions, and your skills have been a marvel to me. As for recognizing you, it was a combination of two things.

"From the moment we arrived I noted some expensive pieces here, yet your behavior would not have met with approval from the kind of people who can afford such things, and so you should have gone out of business as soon as you began. But that only made me wonder. The clue that set me on the right track, well, it was ... your legs."

It was obvious now to everyone. Having once seen legs such as Gettlefinger's—thinner than that of a small child, by half again yet, one would be hard pressed to forget.

Gettlefinger gasped. "It is you who are a marvel. Who are you? No, do not answer. I shall show you the capacity of discernment that I, too, possess. Perhaps not to equal your own, but it has been my very foundation for the thespian craft I so love. Shall I proceed?"

"You may." Mercy retreated half a step behind Fergus.

"I will proceed then. But first excuse me for a moment. I find that I cannot think while I imagine you all staring upon my legs, which no doubt you expect to snap under my ponderous bulk. Lady, you have given me a great gift. This is only the second time that I have worn stockings ... disgusting I'm sure. I shall not make the same mistake again, of that I can assure you."

Gettlefinger ran from the room. But before Fergus could gather his thoughts, even while he was turning to Mercy and constructing words into a question, to his astonishment Gettlefinger was back.

Yet it was not Gettlefinger. At least he was nothing like the man who had just run away.

Gone were the stockings; replaced by heavy leggings. Gone was his middle; it was now slim. Gone were his colorful and bloated garments; now his attire was fitted and grey—even his face was now ashen and drawn. Gone was the foppish demeanor, exchanged for a serious, brooding, yet haughty manner. And there was something else, a slight stumble, a hint of agitation in his chest, and then he coughed. He leaned heavily upon a chair, covering his cough with a white hand-cloth. Slowly the cloth descended away from his mouth as he lowered his hand. There upon it was a spot of blood, and even Gettlefinger's lips were brighter, redder than normal.

Fergus's crew instinctively stepped back.

"Are you sick?" Mercy asked.

He smiled. "I am well. I need but a moment to explain. I was in costume for a new character that I would like to introduce to the city. A friend of mine owns this shop, and he allows me from time to time to use it as a platform for my innovations. Yet you saw through me, and almost immediately. This is a first. For fourteen years no one has guessed at my masquerades. So, I must consider myself a failure or you a genius of greater caliber than even I myself. I prefer to elevate you rather than deprecate me.

"You have undoubtedly come in here to escape the swarming imbeciles out there, and I believe this shop was chosen for no other reason than that it was close at hand when you decided that you had enough of them. Am I correct so far?"

Mercy looked inquiringly at Fergus, who nodded his head in answer.

"Good. Then I am fairly certain of who I have the honor to address." Gettlefinger made an elaborate show of his bow. "Lady Mercy, it would give me great pleasure to see you safely to your destination."

How could he have known? Fergus was feeling most inferior to the circumstances. He simply wished for a foe to stand before him, weapon in hand, declaring in no uncertain terms that he must fight or flee. Somehow Gettlefinger had figured out who Mercy was. Already Fergus had failed in his simple duty—to bring Lady Mercy safe and undetected to the Chronicler. And now, this Gettlefinger fellow had not only detected who she was but seemed to be offering Lady Mercy the very service that Fergus was supposed to be performing.

"But how did you know who I was?" Mercy asked, for she was still shrouded deep within the folds of her cloak.

"There simply wasn't anyone else that made any sense."

"There are thousands of people in the streets today; how can you say such a thing?"

"I shall spell it out for you, and enjoy myself thoroughly in the telling. As everyone knows, Lady Mercy disappeared somewhere between the Hradcanny highway and the river. Her body was never found, and the riders of the hunt reported that she was not seen. So, either the hyenae caused her disappearance or, just as likely, she made it to the river and boarded a ship. It is a mystery that has engaged the collective imagination of this great city.

"Next, this shop is not very far from the docks, and I see that the bottom of your cloak is wet; a likely thing to happen when transferring in and out of a rowing skiff. Also, your manner, your bearing, your speech, the fact that you have three burly escorts, and the fact that you've seen many of my thespian society's plays; it all bespeaks wealth and rank, in a word—nobility."

"But there are many nobles staying aboard their ships, ferrying across the river by skiff."

"Yes, but does the peacock clothe itself in the costume of a pheasant? The pomp of the games is as important to the princes of the realm as are the games themselves. You are clothed as a pheasant, but your beautiful feathers are still apparent to those who are looking. Besides this, your voice and manner also hint at your young age, but where then is your companion? I seldom see ladies of your rank without a female companion by their side. But being rescued from the Queen of Heaven's nonnery and being chased by the Death Hunt hardly gives one time to correct such errors of etiquette.

"In any event, I shall keep your secret. I know that my secret—the discovery of Grimesby to Gettlefinger—will be safe with you. Now, as to my offer of assistance, my cough, the deathly pallor oozing from my pores, and my general appearance of a sickly man is all at your service; I introduce myself as Craven Dregs.

"I can't abide the games for they make it impossible to walk the streets without the populace continually brushing up against me. So I birthed Craven Dregs. Every year at this time, he walks the crowded streets in relative comfort, and he leaves a wake behind him in which you may follow if you like. If you stay far enough behind, no one will notice you, for they will be busy getting out of the way of the sickly, terribly contagious, possibly plague-ridden Craven. It only remains for me to know your destination."

He bowed. He coughed. He bled.

Then attaching the stained hand-cloth to a pole, he staggered into the street. The people gave way before him. And Fergus reluctantly followed Craven Dregs.

Fergus Pulled In

Fergus was lulled into a false sense of security. He had to admit that Craven Dregs was doing a superb job of bringing them through. He also had to admit that he was wrongly upset with the man. It wasn't right for Fergus to find fault in him just because he had succeeded where Fergus had failed. He knew McDougal would have warmly praised Craven for his help, for McDougal enjoyed every minute of someone else's triumphs.

And then it hit him. Maybe Fergus had been so skilled as a shield-bearer only because McDougal had been so skilled as a lord. McDougal, he knew, had been more concerned with Fergus and others than he had been with himself. Even his personal and constant struggle with his awkward and disjointed mannerisms was likely a result of what he knew others wanted and needed from him as their lord.

Fergus glanced back at Mercy. Instead of breeding discontent in his heart by choosing to brood over his own failures, he could instead have chosen to think about the one he was supposed to be serving. She was indeed much more comfortable now … much safer … Fergus turned his heart heavenward and once again told his God that he was sorry.

He thanked Him for Mercy's safety and even for using Craven Dregs to better serve her than he was able to.

A split second before it happened, he knew something was wrong.

The blow took him off his feet; someone in the crowd ran into him when Fergus turned his head to look back at Mercy. He fell hard into Mercy behind him.

He heard her cry out. She fell, and he could do nothing but try and fall over and beyond her, so that he would not crush her small body. In so doing, he had to push off with his feet, and fling himself into Blagger and the messenger beyond. His shame at yet another foolish blunder in his duty turned to rage at what he saw. Rage was an emotion rarely known to Fergus. His controlled demeanor made no room for it, for it meant loss of self-command.

As he came to his feet, he saw a gentleman leaning over Mercy, not to hurt her, but he was offering his hand.

Where was the danger? Who had struck him such a powerful blow?

In an instant he, too, was at Mercy's side. "Are you all right, my Lady?"

She had taken the stranger's hand, and as she rose, Fergus saw the look of pain and the tears brimming.

"I am so sorry, my Lady, please forgive me? I don't know what happened."

"Your incompetence, sir, that is what happened." The stranger turned his head and glared upon Fergus.

Only it wasn't a stranger. And it was definitely not a gentlemen, though he was dressed as one. It was Rush; still sure of himself, still a little black and blue from their last encounter, and still with that devilish gleam in his eye.

"Take your hand from hers," Fergus commanded. His blood raced, and he could barely control himself.

"I am a gentlemen, sir, and I will not be ordered about by a common shield-bearer—oh wait, no, you're not even that anymore."

"I said unhand her. My Lady, let go of his hand, and step behind me."

There were tears now, wetting her cheeks. "I cannot. He holds me tight."

"Dear lady," Rush spoke to Mercy, though he kept his eyes on Fergus, "You will be much safer with me, than with a man who abandons the side of his lord when his lord most needs him."

The rage, the inaction, the mention of McDougal dying without him was more than Fergus could bear. He struck hard with his fist. Rush was armed, but his sword was not drawn. Rush reeled and fell backwards.

He slowly got to his feet. A smile played on his busted lip. That was when Fergus noticed that there were those in the crowd whom he recognized from the night at the Hill Top Inn. And then he saw Aramis, a cold, distant look in his eyes. Two city guards stood alongside.

Rush looked to the guards and pointed at Fergus. "You have seen this gross disregard for the king's law that every man should walk safe upon the king's roads. The law and my honor demand a recompense. As the injured party I offer up a combat of honor."

One of the city guards addressed Fergus. "Do you accept?"

It had been neatly done. He could see this had all been an act—the guards here in the right place at the right time, and Rush baiting Fergus so that he would strike him. He had been pulled in, and there seemed no way to escape it now. "I do."

The guard continued as if he read from a script, for in fact combats of honor were a fairly common way to conclude a quarrel or dispute. "The two combatants cannot see each other again until the combat of honor takes place. Each combatant must elect an agent to represent his interests, to insure that proper protocol is adhered too, and to register the combat. This must be done with the officer of the watch at New-Castle before nightfall, preferably now. I remind both parties that this is a combat of honor, and as such, you are both free to use your time as you see fit, as accords an honorable gentleman, and until the time for the combat can be arranged."

Rush was gloating over his triumph, and even now he looked about for approving nods from his fellow soldiers, and anyone in the crowd who might think to admire him.

"I'd be proud," Blagger said, "to be your agent, Fergus. I've had my hand in a few of these things before, and I know what must be done."

"Thank you, Blagger."

"I'll go with his man now, then," Blagger suggested, "for it looks like their agent's been chosen and is ready. I'll come to the Citadel directly that it's a done thing. Since you struck him and before witnesses, I believe they'll give him the choice of weapons and how the whole thing's to be fought."

"Yes."

"Are there any particular objections I should make on your behalf."

"No, we'll leave it in God's hands."

As Blagger departed, Fergus caught sight of Craven Dregs. He had looped around and was now moving on a path that would intercept Rush. Rush also saw the movement, and then seeing the sickness pole, he immediately quitted his posturing and moved off the street.

"Shall we go, my Lady?" Fergus asked quietly, still feeling his shame.

"Yes, please."

As they walked away from the staring faces, Fergus gave Mercy his arm. "Are you much hurt?" He could hardly ask it without feeling a sting in his own eyes, and he had to swallow almost before he finished the question.

"No. I'm recovered. It mostly startled me. But that man, he scared me very much … and now you must fight him …

and I find that my faith which you and I just recently talked of shall be very much tried. I should not like to have you fall, Fergus Leatherhead."

"No, my Lady, I would not like that either. I will do my best to stand and, God willing, I shall."

The Rules of Engagement

"**L**et me see if I understand you," the Chronicler said, his bushy eyebrows clenched together. "Do you mean to say that her identity and yours have been discovered not once but twice between here and my ship?"

"Yes, sir."

"And that the thespian, Gettlefinger, was one of them, and that you brought him along, that in fact he stands outside my door as we speak?"

"Yes, sir," Fergus said, "Diego Dandolo hustled us in from the alley, and Gettlefinger was, well, hustled in with the rest of us. And when we mentioned who he was, Diego thought it better to bring him along to see what you might want to do with him. Gettlefinger was much impressed with Lady Mercy, and he wanted to do her a service."

"I see. And then someone bumped into you, knocked you down, helped Mercy to her feet, and you struck him a blow with your fist and embroiled yourself in a combat of honor. And that is why Tostig's man is not here right now."

"Yes, sir." That wasn't exactly how Fergus had explained things, and he had not told the Chronicler that Rush would not let go of Mercy's hand, and still more, that he had commanded him twice to unhand the lady. Fergus almost did so now, for he knew it would elevate him some in the eyes of the renowned Chronicler. But no, he would not. He held his tongue as a sort of self-punishment for his failure of duty.

"You've painted a bleak picture of yourself." The Chronicler looked upon him now with eyebrows raised. "Someone used those words to describe me not too long ago. Is there not anything more you can report to me? Everyone else in your party, by your own account, acted most nobly. You even describe your enemy with grace, what was it you said? Oh, yes, 'A slave to his own sin and blackened heart, how could you expect anything more from him? As such only a fool would have been provoked.' You may have acted foolishly, Fergus Leatherhead, but you are no fool."

The Chronicler stood up and stared out the window. Fergus was feeling very small. Again the temptation arose to tell the Chronicler more, but this was only further evidence against him, of how weak a man he truly was.

After a few minutes the Chronicler turned, he even smiled. "Fergus, let's not concern ourselves with what has been. I apologize for my cold reception of your news. It has forced me to change my plans. I was vexed by it, but we must work from where we are, forgetting that which is behind, and pressing on to the goal of the high calling of God. Anyway, it was only a matter of time before our little secrets began to unravel, and we shall use Gettlefinger to our advantage."

"That is very kind of you, sir, too kind."

The Chronicler rang a bell, and almost immediately the door to his room was flung open. Diego Dandolo stepped in, followed by Mercy and Gettlefinger.

"Greetings, Lady Mercy, Grand Thespian Gettlefinger. I will be blunt, for we should move quickly. The king is annoyed that the priests of Bacchus thought to sacrifice you without consulting him first, and the priests of Bacchus are furious that you have been stolen away from them. They have petitioned the king and they want you returned. They go so far as to warn that Bacchus may revenge himself against all who stand in the way of their purposes.

"Do not look so cast down, nay, in all these things we are more than conquerors through Him that loved us. The king does not know where you are, or if he does, he is pretending that he does not. And the whole story of your rescue and the subsequent Death Hunt has so excited the city, that Strongbow, who at first was more than pleased, is now concerned his games will pale in comparison. He is desperate to make these games the very best ever. He will always be swayed by popular opinion, and as long as the buzzing of the people wants to keep Mercy from the hands of the priests then I think we can remove that threat."

"That is where you come in Gettlefinger. How many are there in your thespian society?"

"Close to three score."

"We would like to employ them with the task of spreading Mercy's story while still making the king look very good, and I mean very good. Do you accept this noble charge? And can it be done without delay? Mind you, we want the truth spoken. How shall we expect God's blessing if we dishonor Him with lies."

Gettlefinger bowed first towards Mercy and then towards the Chronicler. "Yes, and yes. Never will a maiden have been so elevated in the minds of men, and what manner of lies could improve upon the truth of this sweet lady?" He bowed yet again, dramatic in the extreme, and then he dashed from the room.

"Now, Mercy," the Chronicler looked upon her with sorrow and kindness, "I do not know what the king shall demand of us. His mind seems less intact than it was even a week ago. You have claimed two men as your champions, one a slave, and one a free man. If Fergus lives through his trial of combat, you must not relinquish him as your man; regardless of the king's feelings on the matter, he must honor your arrangement by law. Therefore if the priests or any other party move against you, we have lawful means to prevent it. Do you understand the importance of this point, Mercy?"

"Yes. But what if uncle sends me back to the nonnery?"

"We shall oppose the move if it comes to that. Just make sure you keep your champions at your side. How does Igi Forkbeard fare?"

"He lost a lot of blood, but his many wounds were mostly superficial, and they are healing fast. He can walk, but not exert himself without dizziness. Maybe he will be well enough tomorrow to travel. If he could be brought upon some conveyance it would help his health, though not his pride."

"Good. Do not concern yourself with the matter; with your permission I will take care of everything."

"Thank you, dear sir. It would be a great blessing to me."

The news soon reached them, upon Blagger's return, that the king himself had left the opening ceremonies to hear first hand from Blagger's lips the story of the morning's events. "His eyes sparkled with merriment, sir, he even clapped me on the back, friendly like. He ordered that the combat would take place in the arena, tomorrow at the second hour past noon; it is to launch tomorrow's games."

"And the combat's particulars?" The Chronicler asked the question that Fergus was eager to know, though he did not want to ask it himself. Somehow he thought it would make him look—and perhaps feel—a more formidable opponent if he appeared as though the choice of weapons and rules of engagement did not matter much to him.

"It is to be rather an unusual contest, sir," Blagger said. "The ingenuity of the thing pleased the king. This fellow

Rush has chosen the hand-crossbow. They are to walk away from each other, twenty paces to the count of a drum; when a gong strikes on the twentieth count, they turn and fire. No armor or any other weapon can be worn. That's it."

The Chronicler turned upon Fergus. "Are you proficient with this weapon?"

"I've some training in the full crossbow, and I am well versed with a long bow."

"Diego, take him to the armory; get what you need, and find a place to practice. Not just with the weapon, but go through the whole contest as it shall be tomorrow, and do it over and over again until dark. Time him against others, pick some men you know to be quick, give him a difficult goal for speed and accuracy. I would like to hear of the results each hour.

"Remember, friends, you all stand here by the grace, mercy, and love of God. Hitherto hath the Lord helped us … raise your eyes heavenward, purpose in your hearts to serve Him with whom we have to do, whatever the cost. Some trust in chariots, and some in horses: but we will remember the name of the Lord our God.

"A horse in battle is a great help to the warrior, but one day the horse will fall, or spook, or throw its rider. It is the same with a man's sword or his own skill with it. One day the sword shall break, or twist free in the warrior's grip, or meet a more skillful or more powerful arm.

"It is in God where our ultimate trust must lie. For even if we do fall, it is a sweet death; a gentle rest in the loving arms of Him who made us. But we do not just walk into battle without our horse or sword and presume upon God that He shall win the day. And we do not enter the field of battle without our God—this is the more dangerous of the two extremes—to be arrogant and prideful in the strength of our own arm and the power of our steed.

"Take a care, my friends. We, too, are expected to play our part, a union of fully trusting in God while working to accomplish the thing we have trusted Him for. So saying, you had better get going, Fergus Leatherhead; for the man you fight, I'm sure, will be skilled with the weapon he has chosen."

Flummery Gate

The night previous had been a difficult one for Count Rosencross—what sleep he found was fitful and plagued with dreams. For he had seen some and heard much of Suzie's little dinner party. He had climbed to the top of the Old City's inner wall, broached the battlements, and crossed them to the crumbling tower that housed Thiery and the rest. He then simply climbed to the rooftop parapet, careful not to make a sound for fear of the wolf's keen ears beneath, and he listened throughout the evening. A couple times he climbed back down, and from a bend of the inner wall battlements, he watched them; actually it was only glimpses of warmth and childish faces but it exerted a powerful sway upon him.

That is where he stood when little Suzie sang. His heart felt strange as he listened and watched the cheery scene. And then when Thiery stood up to recite from the book of Job, Rosencross hurried back to the rooftop where he could hear better; it was a strange sensation that came over him as the words, strong and eloquent, lifted up to his ears and beyond.

He was also moved deeply by the declarations of friendship and loyalty. Rosencross began to remember things, things that he had not wanted to think upon, things he would still try to conceal even from himself. Last night they had broken through unbidden and stirred remorse, a longing to undo the past, maybe even a longing to rectify what he yet could of that past.

And now he sat outside Flummery Gate deep in thought; from a distance he watched the wisp of a child they called Percival. Three boys were speaking to him, but what they said he could not tell. After a few minutes they took the boy's meager earnings from the morning's begging, and then walked him to the center of the plaza. Here the streets converged and widened, and here they left him standing, his head down. It looked like any number of the city's residents would not see him and knock him over as they passed.

Even after the boys left the plaza, Percival kept his place. The minutes passed to an hour and still he would not move. Once he was pushed aside by some inconsiderate merchant, but the child quickly recovered, and again took his place exactly in the center of the bustling goings on.

A cry of alarm issued forth from some panicked citizen on the other side of Flummery Gate. A moment later there was the sound of pounding hooves and people scattered to make way for the horseman. But the child still did not move.

Rosencross had convinced himself that he would let things happen as they would with the little boy. It was just the way he might feel about a weak or sickly deer being culled by a pack of wolves. That is why he had not interfered when the older boys had stolen his money. But this time, he involuntarily rose from his seat and took a step towards Percival, almost calling his name, almost warning him to get out of the way.

In an instant, he realized it would come too late; he stared upon the scene as the horse rode the boy down.

The flashing hooves echoed off store fronts, and others too saw what must unfold, turning open mouths, too late to grab the boy out of harm's way. It was over in a second; the horse and rider were gone.

Still standing in the street was little Percival, shaking violently, but still standing. His knees buckled once and then twice, but both times he recovered himself, and stood ... he stood. The horse had missed him by a hand's span or less. Tremendous, explosive muscles had pounded and even shook the earth where he stood. It had charged past, so very near him, and he still had not moved.

Rosencross began to grow quite curious about the boy. Why did he stand exactly in the center of the Plaza? And what made such a young, sickly thing stand so resolutely?

Then a new rousing swept the crowds. A town crier placed a crate not far from Percival and leapt upon it. The masses rushed in and Percival disappeared amid the tumult.

"Do you want to hear what has occurred so far this day?" The crier bellowed.

"Yes!" The crowd roared in return.

"A man breathed fire. Another swallowed a sword. And yet a third rode upon the back of a dragon!"

The crowd was almost silent now, their awe apparent from the quiet gasps, the wide eyes, the stillness of their limbs.

"I must hurry, though, my friends, there are so many tales yet to tell. And I must hurry back and see what transpires."

A moan of disappointment gushed from the people.

"But before I do," said the crier, "would you like to hear what happened with the giants?"

The crowd broke into a frenzy. "Yes!" A hundred arms shot into the air, cheering. The cobbles they stood upon were ground and stamped by two-hundred feet. Could the little beggar possibly have kept to the center? Or even kept his feet?

"Three giants, by the names of Ogre, Lunace, and Goblin, are the fiercest men you ever did see. They wield weapons capable of dropping buildings to their knees. Our fiercest dragon, raised for seventy-years, fell before them. Enraged, six Dragon Priests and four heroes jumped into the arena, only to fall before the giants three. They challenge us, people of Hradcanny, people who follow Strongbow; they mock us. Will there be a champion who can best them, and take our honor back? Besides this, did you know that the lands of Lord McDougal have been conquered?"

A gasp.

"And who do you suppose it was that took that part of our kingdom?"

The people cried out, "Who?"

"Giants!"

Another gasp. And then the town crier leapt down, grabbed his crate, and ran. The people dispersed, talking, grinding teeth, clenching fists, and abhorring the giants.

As the plaza held fewer and fewer people, Rosencross kept his eyes upon where Percival had been. As he did so, he rose, and walked to the center, glancing this way and that, wondering what had become of the little fellow. The commotion had left a few articles behind. A shawl, some discarded slops, and only a bit larger ... a pile of garbage. The garbage moved, it coughed, and coughed, and coughed. Then it lay perfectly still.

Rosencross stepped closer and saw the closed eyes of the little beggar, his torn clothes, rags really, his bruised and dirty face, and he thought the boy must be hours or perhaps minutes from death's door. Percival had received a terrible drubbing from the crowd; the Count thought it too bad they had not stilled his heart quicker; he looked a sad and broken sight.

Suddenly, the wide eyes of the child flitted open. They were clear, bright, and very much alive. "Did God send you?" his voice squeaked.

The Count just stared.

"Are you a giant?"

"No."

"You're very big."

"I suppose. Not nearly as big as a giant."

"Oh ... did God send you to me?"

"I don't know what you mean."

"Not the wood kind or the stone kind," Percival said, grunting as he stood up. He dusted himself off, and regained the center of the plaza. "You know, the big one we can't see ... Noah's God. I never heard much 'bout him till last night, and now I want to know more ... and I just asked that great big invisible God of Noah for some help and when I opened my eyes you was standing there."

"Hmmm."

"Thiery, he's my new friend, he says the wood and stone kind aren't even real ... oh, but I guess you knew that."

"I know no such thing."

"Really?"

"Really."

"That's strange." Percival looked up into the Count's face, tilting his head one way and then another, "Oh well. I'm sure God knows why he sent you then. You're big enough to help me. But your face is kinda, kinda, well ... not friendly. You didn't come to do me harm, did ya?"

"Of course not." Rosencross wasn't even sure why he was talking to the little bit of rags.

"I didn't think so. Well, what should we do next?"

"What are you talking about, Percival?"

Percival's eyes widened, and then a big grin spread across his cheeks, dimpling them through the smudges. His eyes sparkled. "I knew it!"

"Knew what? Can't you speak with more sense?"

"I knew that God sent you to help me."

"What makes you so sure? I think it a very dubious proposition."

"I don't know about a dubilus propalisten. But God must have sent you because you knew my name. How else could you know my name? Did you know that I am brave too?"

"Hmmm." The Count was not about to tell him how it was he knew his name—how he had been sneaking about and spying in the dark last night. "I could not decide if you were addled in your head or if you were brave ... my curiosity has gotten the better of my good sense it seems. Okay then, why did you not move when the horse rode past or when the crowd trampled you?

"Because I was being brave."

"It's not bravery," Rosencross explained, extremely annoyed, "to stand by and let yourself be run over when you could have simply moved out of the way."

"But I couldn't move."

"And why not?"

"Because something bad will happen."

"Can't you try and explain things more fully. It almost seems like you are trying to exasperate me. What is the bad thing that you are afraid of? This time tell me everything."

Percival looked confused. "I can't."

"Why?"

"I don't know what eggs purrate means. Is it some kind of food? Pip says I'll eat anything."

"Just tell me what the bad thing is."

"Okay. Pip and I got a three-day scolding from Master Squilby. There's two days left but Pip went to the Citadel with Thiery this morning. Thiery wants a place there, and Pip and I mean to help him, because he's our new friend, and he's got a sister to take care of. She's real nice, really, really nice. I like her a lot. Am I makin' sense so far?"

Rosencross nodded his head.

"I don't know what happened," Percivial continued, "but some sneaks came and said I couldn't beg anymore, and I'm not protected no more by Master Squilby, and Pip's not a sneak no more. Then Bully said I had to stand in this spot until Pip came for me, and if I didn't move then they wouldn't be too hard on him, but if I moved then Pip might not come back at all. So I'm being brave for my brother. Did I make some more sense for you?"

"Better."

"So what are you going to do?" Percival asked. "Can you help my brother and bring him back here to me so I can move from this spot? I don't think any bunch of sneaks would try scrappin' with you. And I'm gettin' real tired and hungry."

"I'm not for interfering," Rosencross said, "where things don't concern me. But I have an interest in speaking with the boy, Thiery."

Percival squinted his eyes and chewed on the inside of his lip. "I don't understand much of what you say either. Does that mean a yes or a no to helpin' me?"

Count Rosencross laughed, and then he turned and walked away without a word.

The Oracles

The Citadel had many wondrous sights within its walls, and Thiery could hardly believe that he was on his way to becoming one of its apprentices. There were not many honors greater than to have been trained at the Citadel.

Pip directed him through the commons—a massive chamber filled with an assortment of warriors and scholars, young and old—they were talking and studying, intent upon the purposes their duties imposed. They all waited for the afternoon hour when the games would begin and they would be allowed to attend. Some present would even participate. Thiery and Pip made their way to a corner table, half concealed behind a marble pillar.

Besides the excited tension caused by the nearness of the games, a thing most perceptible, there was something else about this place which made it singularly strange. It was a tendency, an inclination, an unconscious habit common to everyone present. Quick glances, or lingering gazes travelling up the wide, rounded stairs—thirty steps in all—atop which was a dais high upon the stone wall, to the place of the Oracles. There was no door up there, no hallway, no window; it was stark without ornament except for the Oracles—three faces cut into the stone, with black hollow eyes and open mouths.

"When will they call me?" Thiery asked.

"Whenever they feel like it. They might not call you at all today." Pip said.

"But the attendant said there weren't any other requests pending. Doesn't that mean we should be next?"

"Most likely, but next could be tomorrow, or the day after, or even longer. There must be three of the Citadel's masters to question you behind those masks and many will be busied by the games. But that means there'll be less requests to speak with them, as we've seen by your being the only one so far this morning. You'll just have to be patient, my friend." Pip stiffened.

"What is it?" Thiery asked.

"I just saw a sneak. He saw us and took off. I was hoping we'd not be noticed. Now that they have though, Bully will hear of it, and I'll have to bear up under his provokin' ways."

"Maybe you should leave, then. I don't want to get you in any kind of trouble. And didn't Master Squilby say you couldn't come back for three days?"

"Leave you? Leave you! What kind of friend do you take me for? I guess you just don't think that highly of me is all. Well, just to show ya what kind of friend I am, I'm gonna turn the other cheek and not take offense at those offendin' words of yours, and maybe one day you'll think more proper like, about me and Percival." Pip looked every which way except at Thiery. "This not takin' offense stuff is awful hard. I hope you ain't often the offending type."

"I didn't mean anything by it Pip. Can't I be a friend to you by looking out for your interests above my own? That's all I was trying to do. If all I cared about was myself, then I'd much rather have you here with me."

"Oh … never thought about it that way … that even makes a heap of sense. I'll just thicken up my skin a bit."

Bully soon sauntered up to the table. A bunch of sneaks followed behind, fanned out, and surrounded them. One sat down on either side of Pip and two more did the same with Thiery. The rest stood, casual, and acting friendly. But there was something tense about them hovering so close, and Thiery remembered how it was just before they pounced on him during Squilby's interview. But what would they dare to do here in the open, before scribes, and warriors, and the Oracles?

"We're takin' Bard's dagger back," Bully said, sticking out his chest and looking mean. "Hand it over."

Thiery ignored him and looked over at Bard. "I don't know why he's so riled, Bard, but I told him to tell you the dagger was yours and I'd be happy to return it. It seems like Bully didn't give you the message the way I intended it, or perhaps he couldn't understand me. But here you go. No hard feelings, I hope."

"That's right," Pip said, "That's exactly the way it happened. Thiery here's a real good one for bein' true and straight."

Bully's face was growing crimson. "Remember, boys, what he said about our gods. And remember how displeased Master Squilby was. And you better keep your mouth shut, Pip. Unless it's like we've been thinkin', that you're not one of us any more, seeing how you let the Green Archer pummel us without so much as a warning. And now you're pretty friendly with this guy. It doesn't look good to Master Squilby, either."

Bully gained confidence as the rest of the sneaks began to nod their heads; he turned back to Thiery. "We didn't come just for the dagger. Give us Master Squilby's endorsement."

"What do you mean? I earned it."

"We're earning it back," Bully sneered. "Pip, this is your chance to show us who you're with. Tell him to hand it over."

Pip hesitated; he looked around at his fellow sneaks, but they mostly averted their eyes.

Bully put both his hands on the table and leaned in front of Pip's face. "Come on, Pip. Are you still a sneak or not?"

Pip sighed. "Thiery's my friend, and I'd sooner cross fists with you than turn my back on him."

"You heard him boys. We know what's what now. How 'bout you Thiery, are you gonna hand it over?"

"You know I won't ..." Thiery had more to say, but before he could the sneaks on either side grabbed his arms, and to his surprise someone under the table grabbed his legs. Pip was subdued in the same way. No matter how hard he tried, he couldn't budge, and it would have taken a keen eye for anyone in the hall to notice what was happening, so smooth and quick were their movements. Within a few seconds they had rifled through his garments, and one of the sneaks waved his endorsement in front of his face, before handing it over to Bully.

Bully pocketed the tin piece and smiled. "Don't think of making a fuss over this. You sure don't want to cause a commotion in here and lose any chance you might still have of joining this grand institution, do you?"

It was Thiery's turn to grow red, but he could see that Bully was right—there was nothing to be gained through a struggle now. He calmed, and the sneaks let him go.

Thiery closed his eyes and bowed his head. He half expected the sneaks to have wandered silently away as he prayed, but when he opened his eyes, they were all there, strange looks upon their faces.

"What did you just do?" Bully whispered.

"I was praying."

"Praying what?"

"I did want to pray that God would give you what you deserve. But instead I asked Him to save you."

"Save me? What are you talking about? Save me from what?" Bully tried to say it with bravado, but it was obvious by his stilted manner that he felt some apprehension.

"From Hell, Sheol, the place of gnashing teeth and darkness, Bully. I don't want you to go there, nor any of your friends."

The sneaks began to inch away. Even Pip looked alarmed.

"Huh, don't bother with me. Come on, boys," Bully said, "we got things to do yet this morning. And Pip, I don't know what Master Squilby's gonna say about all this, but you better stay away from me. Better watch your back cause we ain't gonna." And quick as can be they withdrew.

"Sorry, Pip," Thiery said, "I've brought you a lot of trouble."

Pip tried to look unconcerned, but his smile seemed forced. "No, no, don't say that. I'm sure Master Squilby won't expel me. And anyway, if he does, it only takes one other master to agree to my staying and then I can continue on here at the Citadel. Why just a few days ago the Chronicler's assistant said as I had potential and all. I'd just not be a sneak anymore."

"Well, I'm glad there's hope then. But I am sorry for my part."

"None of it. But what of you? They've done taken away your chance. What'll you do now?"

Just then a hush fell over the hall, and all heads turned to the Oracles.

Candlelight danced in the eyes of the middle mask.

Thiery gulped, hoping now that they wouldn't call his name.

The voice from the Oracle was loud and commanding, "Thiery, recommended by Master Squilby ... approach!"

The occupants of the hall were looking about.

"What should I do, Pip?"

"You'll have to go up there, and hurry!"

"But I don't have my recommendation."

"Just get goin', it seems to me that it would be a lot worse to sit and pretend they aint callin' you."

And so Thiery stood. Everyone turned to stare. He walked amongst the tables, thinking of what he should say. He slowly climbed the steps, still trying to think of a suitable explanation. And then he stood before the three stone masks—the Oracles—and his heart pounded.

Crack Brained Crazy

"What happened?" Pip asked in hushed tones.

"I'm not exactly sure."

"What do ya mean? Wha'd they say?"

"They asked me to give them my recommendation, and of course I couldn't. I thought it better not to say who it was who took it from me, so I just told them the story of how I got Master Squilby's piece of tin in the first place, and how I was let in to see them, and then that it was stolen."

"Didn't they want to know who took it?"

"I guess not. They were quiet; I heard some whispering, but nothing I could make out. And then they asked me what I thought would happen by the end of the games. Would the giants prevail? Or would the men of Hradcanny?"

"Wha'd they ask that for?"

"Yeah, it confused me too. But I composed myself and I was figuring out what I thought they would like to hear … just in time though, I thought of what my God would prefer me to say."

Pip's mouth dropped open. "What did your God want you to say?"

"I don't know for sure," Thiery said. "but I told them that 'Even God who quickeneth the dead, and calleth those things which be not as though they were—He knows the end from the beginning—and as far as the giants were concerned, I couldn't possibly know."

Pip's mouth dropped open further. "Wow, that sounds mighty fine. Wha'd they say to that?"

"They were quiet for a while. I think they whispered some more, and then the candles were placed back into the center mask, just as you saw, and I guess they left."

"Gone? They didn't say anything else?" Pip threw up his arms.

"Nothing. I waited a few minutes, and when they didn't say anything, I turned around and came back here."

"Wow," Pip said, "I wonder what it means."

"Me too. I guess there's nothing left to do but get going then."

"Oh no! Not while the candle's burning, they might call you back up there; it wouldn't do for you to leave now." Pip started chewing on the inside of his lip. "How come you keep bringin' your God into everything?"

Thiery smiled. "Precisely because He is God."

"Yeah, but, I mean, you talked about Him a lot last night, which was fine, in fact I found it real interestin', but you made Master Squilby real mad with talk of Him. I know Bard didn't like it, and I think you might have done the same thing just now with the Oracles ... I mean, shouldn't you keep quiet about your God when you think it'll get you in trouble?"

"It is true that the Lord's people have been threatened not to speak of Him, held in derision, mocked, or given council as you have just done—to at least keep quiet concerning Him, but you be the judge, whether it be right in the sight of God to hearken unto you more than to God. For God would have me speak; woe is unto me, if I preach not.

"Once, I said in my heart, I will not make mention of Him, nor speak any more in His name. But His word was in my heart as a burning fire shut up in my bones, and I was weary with forbearing, and I could not stay … my mouth … I could not keep my mouth closed any longer."

Pip's eyes were wider than Thiery had ever seen them. "A burning fire in your bones?"

They talked some during the long wait, but mostly they watched the candles burn; ever lower, for hours, they watched the candles burn. Pip fidgeted every few minutes, followed by sighs and exclamations of discontent. Thiery also found it difficult to wait, especially when it was uncertain whether or not it was necessary to wait at all.

Suddenly, Pip jumped to his feet. "They're out. I thought it would never end. I never was good at waiting; give me something to do and I'm okay, but make me sit still for ten minutes and I feel like I'm dyin' here."

Thiery laughed. "Your brother must be getting awfully hungry by now. Shall we go collect him? I'm anxious to get home to Suzie and hear how Gimcrack did. I hope he fared better than us."

They traveled an unusually circuitous route of side streets and alleys. Pip was not his talkative self, and he was more taut than normal. But Thiery hadn't known him long, and he thought it possible that Pip was just thinking on the day's events and the conversation between them. So that by the time they were approaching Flummery Gate Thiery had lulled himself into his own thoughts and was startled by Pip's sigh. "Well that wasn't easy, but I think we've evaded their traps."

"Traps?" Thiery asked.

"Yep, I kept spotting the signs of it before we sprung'em though. Sneaks were trying to get us. But they wanted it to be a startlin' thing, and they knew I knew each time they were about to try, and so we got away with it. I think they gave up for today."

"I didn't see anything." Thiery looked around at the many people flitting about, and decided to look a little more suspiciously upon every nook and cranny; any place where a sneak might be hidden.

Pip cried out, "Oh no, he's gone! Percival's gone! They wouldn't dare do anything to him."

Just then a little voice called, "Pip! Pip!"

Thiery and Pip spun around in the direction of the sound, but the plaza was wide and filled with hectic activity—they strained to hear, but nothing was forthcoming.

They strode almost to the plaza's center; Pip called for his brother.

No response. A city guard stood nearby, solidly built, his legs spread, and his halberd held menacingly. It seemed he was ready to defend his position from the bustling crowd—not actually attacking anyone, but making them keep their distance. At his feet was poor little Percival, clutching some sort of bundle; he was convulsed in one of his coughing fits and yet he tried to cry out, but he could not.

Pip tried to go to Percival's side but the guard blocked his path. "Step around boy; on your way with you."

"But, sir, he's my brother, won't you please let me to him."

"Excellent!" the guard said, completely changing his manner. "If you see the nobleman who set me here, make sure you tell him I did my duty by him." The man jingled his purse. "And I'll gladly serve him again in future, don't forget now, let him know what I said." Before either of them could answer, he merged into the crowd and was soon out of sight.

Pip lifted his brother into his arms and rocked him until the coughing subsided. His face was paler than usual, and when Thiery reached out to touch his hands, they were so very cold.

Percival smiled weakly; his eyes seemed a bit glassy. "Can we stay at their home again tonight?" His voice was quiet, but Thiery overheard the gist of the question. Thiery and

Gimcrack had discussed the matter that morning. They wondered where the boys slept, and it threatened to be cold again this night. Gimcrack had given Thiery permission to invite the boys to stay with them if their own quarters seemed inadequate. Pip looked uncomfortable.

"Of course you're coming home with us," Thiery said. "I mean if you want to. Suzie will be awfully disappointed if I show up without you."

"Did you hear that Pip? They want us." Percival looked up hopefully.

A tear rolled down Pip's cheek. "We'd better not disappoint Suzie then. Thanks Thiery, we'll never forget your kindness to us ..." Pip's shoulders shook some, and for a long time nobody spoke. Pip tried to stop his tears. Percival reached a little hand up and wiped them away whenever one escaped. People continued to walk past them, hurrying and bustling about their lives.

"I had a brave day." Percival squeaked.

"You must have; what happened?" Pip seemed to relax some, but his anxiety was still evident.

"Bully came and said I couldn't beg anymore. He said I wasn't protected by Master Squilby no more either. Then they said I had to stay in the center here or you might never come back. So you know I wouldn't move. I didn't move even when a horse almost stomped me. And then a big crowd came and they did stomp me, but I still didn't move. What's wrong Pip? Why do you look like that?"

"It's nothing, go ahead."

"Then I did something I never did before. I asked Thiery's God to help me. I kept my eyes closed like Thiery does, and I talked to Him in my head—like I was thinkin', only I was thinkin' to Him."

"What happened?" Pip set Percival down and they began their walk home.

"Well I was pretty excited because nobody stepped on me for a while, and then I decided to open my eyes."

"Yeah?" Pip was strung up again, like a bow about to fire.

"There was a big, big, big man standin' over me."

"Go figure! That city guard?"

"Nope. A bigger, bigger, bigger man. And he knew my name!" Percival and Pip were working themselves into a contagious excitement that made Thiery smile as he watched.

"No!" Pip slapped his leg.

"Yep!" Percival slapped his leg too.

"You're sure he knew your name?"

"Yep." And Percival slapped his leg again for good measure.

"Well, I say, that's a mighty fine story."

"Yep, and there's more. Then the man left and a little while later that guard came to protect me, and he handed me this here sack. Guess what's in it?"

"Gold!" Pip exclaimed.

Percival started laughing until the tears came. "That's a good one Pip ... gold ... ha ha he he ... you're so funny. You're the best brother ever."

"Well, what's in there then, it looks like a real nice bag, and big too."

"Yep, and there's some food in here, so we can do our part at dinner. Two loaves of bread, some beans, and apples, and .... what I think is a jacket, a real fine jacket, and some shoes."

"You don't say. Let's put that jacket on you. It'll warm you up good."

"Oh no, I can't"

"Why not?"

"Cause."

"Cause why?"

"Cause you don't have one, Pip. It wouldn't be fittin'."

"Why you crack brained crazy in the bug house." Pip said as he jabbed a finger in Percival's ribs. "Don't you know that whatever good comes your way is good that comes mine, too? I'll feel warmer just knowin' that you are, besides the cold doesn't bother me like it does you."

Percival was giggling. "Crack brained crazy in the bug house ... I like it when you say that."

So they tucked little Percival into the jacket, and everyone smiled.

"Say it again, Pip?" Percival looked up at his brother admiringly.

Pip accentuated each word to Percival's utter delight. "Crack brained crazy in the bug house."

That night, snug in the old tower, the small party shared with each other their day's happenings; they praised God, and were joyful in their togetherness. Unknown to them, an evil lurked nearby. Once again, they were watched. This time there were three of them.

The malodorous Flemup and Elvodug, thrilled to be free from their cookery, and a red robed priest.

"Do you understand me?" The priest said to Elvodug, his long blue fingers pointing towards the children inside; his nasal voice was stern and slimy.

"Yes. Get her without anyone else the wiser. Bring her to you, and we're not to let the Count know about it either. And then you'll give us that bag of silver." Elvodug shuddered as the blue tattooed finger swung round and hovered near his face.

"Remember," The priest crooned, "she must disappear without a trace. Be patient until the time is right. She must be alone. And do not think of betraying this charge, for we priests of the Dragon are many, and we have our ways."

Just then, as the two thieves were feeling the fear of the priest's words, and the priest seemed to be relishing in the power he held over them, Suzie's voice gently pierced their dark conspiring.

The priest's hood twisted toward the small light of the tower window-slit and the beautiful voice within. The thieves froze.

For I will declare mine iniquity;
I will be sorry for my sin.

But mine enemies are lively, and they are strong:
And they that hate me wrongfully are multiplied.
They also that render evil for good are mine adversaries;
Because I follow the thing that good is.

Forsake me not, O LORD:
O my God, be not far from me.
Make haste to help me, O Lord my salvation.
Let not the hand of the wicked remove me.

There are the workers of iniquity fallen:
They are cast down, and shall not be able to rise ...

The words of wrath-upon-the-wicked mixed with such a sweet and innocent voice held an eerie quality for the men of wickedness who listened. The rest of the song, which spoke of praise to God, His mercies and grace, and His calling, ever calling to the sinners come home, were lost upon their darkened hearts.

The priest turned and walked away.

Flemup found his voice first. "Why must she always sing those terrible songs?" He whispered, "It's like she knows what we're thinking better than we do. Almost like she even knows we're out here now."

"It's your own fault!" Elvodug whispered back.

"My fault?"

"Yes, you barmy fool. You should have made her stop when she was littler."

"Me? Her songs make me feel strange inside, uneasy, like I might get struck by lightning if I touched a hair on her head." Flemup looked bewildered, then indignant. "You could have made her stop, your own blabby fool self could have done it, that's right, done it your own self. Besides it was you that got her that nurse who taught her all that evil sounding caterwauling; that was the dumbest, stupidest, brainless dim-witted scheme you, your own barmy fool self, came up with."

Elvodug prepared a powerfully mean retort, something to really blast Flemup with, something genius like. But the more he thought about it, the more the fire in his chest, the pounding in his temples, and the clenching of his fists subsided; that nurse had ruined everything.

"For the first time in your life, Flemup, I think you're right. Just don't let it go to your muddle brained head, you barmy blabby fool."

So the two thieves sat down to conspire.

The occasional song, those that esteemed the narrow way and called out God's wrath upon the wide way that leads to destruction, would drift across the cool night air. The thieves would shift and turn and even shiver, until Elvodug came up with an idea. It was the first idea that they both could agree upon. Smiling with glee, the fools plugged their fingers into their ears, refusing to listen as wisdom cried at the gates, at the entry of the city, at the coming in at the doors.

Combat of Honor

The arena was elliptical in shape, sunken deep into the earth and surrounded by an amphitheater climbing seventy feet into the air from the city streets; but from the sunken arena floor to the top of the amphitheater was a full one-hundred-feet. The floor was made of fat oaken planks, beneath which were many more levels of subterranean vaults and passages, from which all manner of spectacular beasts could be raised to the arena floor as if they had been birthed by the earth itself. Whole sections of flooring could be removed to reveal man-made tar pits, bogs, and witty inventions—including traps. Around the arena's perimeter was a wide ditch that could be filled with water, upon which boat races and mock sea-battles took place.

It seemed that King Strongbow created more, spent more, and killed more every year. It was a path that did not seem sustainable. But the people grew to expect and lust after it, and so Strongbow became consumed by its pursuits.

The immense structure was six-hundred-feet long and five-hundred-feet wide, built with ever narrowing tiers of stone—four levels all together. Under each tier were colonnades and galleries, stairs, vaulted chambers, stone columns and arches, and public privies that joined to the city sewers, employing scores of night-soil workers.

The face of each tier began at its lowest point as a balcony or parapet that rose back as a slope of benches until it reached the next tier. Thirty to forty-thousand people could sit and watch the games, not nearly enough to satisfy the city; especially since the entire first balcony was reserved for the king, his nobles, princes from other lands, high priests of the different gods, and the vestals of the Queen of Heaven. The tier rising behind it was reserved for the higher classes: warriors of position, scholars, and traders. The second and third tiers were meant for the rank and file of the city.

The king sat elevated upon his royal platform; two warriors flanked him, and two scribes flanked them, busily writing down the conversations upon the dais and the activities of the arena. The queen and Princess Catrina were near, but not so near as the witch Esla.

Strongbow raised his arm, a red cloth in his fingers.

The voices of the amphitheater became a quiet hum, then a whisper, and then silence.

A trap door opened over one of the arena's pits. A cow was raised, and a priest began the sacrificial ceremony that would open the day's games.

Fergus and Blagger stood behind one of four portcullises that led into the arena; they were watching and waiting for their gate to rise. Fergus would then walk by himself to the table at the arena's center, where two hand-crossbows were waiting, where the Master of Games waited, and where Rush would soon be.

Fergus felt a fear like he had never known before. It was not for himself that he feared, and it was not like the fear he had felt for Lord McDougal in times past. Lady Mercy and her safety were now his responsibility, he feared that he would fail her, that he would die in a senseless duel, and she would not have the protection which she needed. He knew there were others, like Igi Forkbeard and the Chronicler who would try, would they try as much as he? Would they give their lives solely for her? Fergus could only doubt that they would; the Chronicler had many others to think of, and Igi was an unknown. His duty to another god or to self might get in the way of his duty to Mercy. And so he felt the weight of this combat upon his shoulders.

"Fergus," Blagger said, clearing his throat, "I've been thinking about all your practicing yesterday."

"I know." Fergus needn't say more, for he had demonstrated himself to be only average with the weapon as far as speed was concerned. He never missed his mark, but the spinning around, grabbing the crossbow that dangled from a cord at his belt, getting his finger around the trigger without pulling too soon, aiming, and then firing, had proved a most difficult procedure. Six of the ten men that he had practiced with were faster than he was.

"We can only assume Rush is exceedingly fast, would you not agree, Fergus?"

"Is this speech meant to strengthen my courage, friend?"

Blagger grinned. "I'm sorry, no, I only mean to suggest a different strategy. You were much faster the other way, and I think it is your only chance."

Fergus was quiet. He had been thinking the same thing. Only the 'other way' was more difficult, and he had only been successful with it on every third try, but when the maneuver worked he easily beat his opponents.

The rules of the contest required that the crossbow hang on the opposite side of the body from the trigger finger—one end of a string tied to the crossbow and one end tied to a ring, looped over a belt peg; the ring sliding free when the weapon was lifted. So Fergus must reach across with his right hand to the crossbow on his left side, fumble for a second to get his grip, and place his finger inside the trigger mechanism, all while he raised it to a firing position. The spinning action of his body actually caused the weapon to rotate freely in the air; if he allowed his leg to make contact with the crossbow, more often than not it would catch and spin violently, making an effectual grab almost impossible.

Yet they had found that if Fergus spun around the opposite way using his trigger side as the axis for his turn, a way that seemed desperately counterintuitive, then he could come to bear much quicker. The problem being that his weapon was on the wrong side of his body to make this tactic feasible.

But, if with his left hand he sent the crossbow flinging behind him, the string connected to his belt peg would cause the crossbow to arc and then fly into the air as it released from his belt—he could then still spin round on his trigger side and the crossbow, if it had been thrust back with the correct force, could be caught up and fired. There were indeed more variables to go wrong; the chief one being the catching of a weapon in mid-air just after whirling round.

Blagger was right though, it was likely his only chance, unless God was to supernaturally speed up his own hand or slow the hand of Rush. Of course, Fergus must run to the arms of His God and trust in His might. At the same time he must do, with what God had given him, all that he could. Therein lies peace for the soul.

The moment he thought of His God, it struck him that it was his pride that was stopping him from using the 'other way', for if he missed he would look foolish; he would die looking foolish.

The Master of Games said something, but Fergus, lost in thought, didn't hear. The sacrifice was over and the portcullis began to rise.

"God bless you, Fergus, my prayers go with you."

"Thanks, Blagger, God bless." Fergus walked into the arena.

Rush stepped out from an entrance on the opposite side.

The portcullises closed behind them.

The Master of Games stood behind the large table; he raised his arms dramatically in welcome to the two combatants. "Lay down your weapons, goodmen. Swords, daggers, your spear, sir, and anything else upon your persons. Take up a crossbow and load."

Rush disarmed, grabbed his weapon, and loaded well before Fergus had. He could feel the eyes of Rush upon him, and so he took his time, looking over the firing mechanism, raising and lowering the nut, and then he pulled back the cord and secured it. Placing his bolt he looked up, first at Rush, and then to the Master of Games.

Rush's cold eyes had been locked upon him. Fergus saw the hate and loathing in his young face, but there had been something more. It seemed to Fergus that Rush was questioning, concerned perhaps that he would not be fast enough. The look was fleeting though, and it was quickly replaced with his usual arrogance.

"Goodmen, I will retreat to the safety of yonder barricade. You shall place your backs to each other now ... good. The drummer shall give the beat. With each strike you shall take a step away. After ten paces, but before twenty, a gong shall ring. The gong is your signal to turn and fire. You may not reach for your weapons, nor may you turn, until you hear the gong; to do so will mean your death. Is this understood? Good. Remember, this is a combat of honor. Once both bolts have been fired, the contest is over. Honor is served regardless of the outcome. Is this understood? Good. I retire then."

It was strange to stand back to back, so close to the young man who hated him. Fergus felt no hatred or even anger towards Rush. He did not want to kill him, fight him, or have anything whatsoever to do with him, yet here they were about to exchange blows; blows that would likely end in the death or serious wounding of one or the other. What was it in man that caused such quarrels? Pride certainly, and a deceitful, wicked heart. In short, the fallen condition of man … without God. Rush was without God, a young man barely older than a boy who was hastening towards hell; and Fergus might send him there with the pull of a trigger …

Thrum—the first drumbeat pulsed.

Fergus took a step.

Thrum—another pulse, and then a third.

Fergus had fought in many battles, facing men who he had not known. Duty had called him to fight for his lord, for the land and its peoples, for the ladies and the children—but seeing men die had never lost its horror for him.

Thrum. Thrum. Thrum.

Oh God! I do not want to kill this man, and thereby send his soul on its way …

Thrum. Thrum.

But did his duty not call him to fight this duel? Was it not a trap that Rush himself had laid for him? Yes, and Fergus had been foolish enough to fall prey to it. But now that he had, should he not raise his arm in defense? The alternative was to stand and die.

Thrum. Thrum. Thrum. Thrum …

He had lost count. Could the gong ring now? He must be ready. And then it did—like a thunderclap.

Fergus no longer thought. He reacted as a warrior.

He thrust the crossbow behind him with his left hand, as he spun to the right. The ring scraped along its peg. As he came around the weapon hovered at the apex of its climb, just before it would begin its descent back to the ground. For a second it hung perfectly in the air, upright, level, and pointed where it should.

Fergus plucked it deftly from the air, resting the stock in his palm, and pulled. Part of him waited for the impact of Rush's bolt, and part of him watched to see Rush fall to the ground.

Neither happened.

The last of the gong's metallic humming ebbed into quiet. The host of hungry onlookers was hushed. Fergus' eyes focused on Rush's crossbow; the cord was no longer pulled back. The bolt was gone. And then he saw the small cloud of dust very close by; caused by Rush's bolt, stuck in the wooden floor of the arena just a few cubits from the feet of Fergus.

Rush had pulled the trigger as he raised his weapon, and therefore fired too early. He had been too fast, too quick to pull; perhaps unnerved as he saw how speedily Fergus was coming to bear.

But then where was the bolt of Fergus's weapon? Had he too missed?

And then he realized that his finger was outside the trigger housing and that he had not fired at all. Rush lowered his arms, stuck out his chest, and glared defiantly.

Fergus turned his eyes heavenward. You heard my cry oh God, thank you! And then he too aimed his crossbow into the wooden planks at their feet and fired.

Immediately the crowds came to life, some animated with cheers and some with a jeering hiss. Fergus turned towards the king and bowed. As he rose, the crowd took up a different sound, the meaning of which Fergus could not comprehend. Then the full impact of its cause was thrust upon him.

For Rush had already reached the table. He caught up his sword, and with a menacing smile turned on Fergus.

Death Comes Quickly

S omeone shouted an order for Rush to desist. If the order was repeated it could not be heard amid the roar of the crowd, for now they jumped to their feet and seemed a frenzied mass of yelling faces and waving arms.

Rush was moving towards him. He too was saying something, but again the clamor of the entertained mob masked whatever it was. Rush was not offering Fergus a weapon to defend himself; the combat of honor was over, and murder had begun.

Fergus could run away, but to what end? To be chased and cut down from behind? No, he would wait until the last minute, and hope for a surprise. Rush just might look to the pleasure of the crowds, to bask in their admiration before dealing his deathblow. That would be when Fergus would act.

Rush was a scant two paces away from Fergus when he raised his sword. His stare was intensely fixed upon Fergus' eyes.

Another step, and still his eyes did not move. His shoulders twisted slightly, his sword arm raised yet further, and then his muscles bunched just before the strike. A flutter of movement, a wisp of air, a strange crunch or grating of bone; and Rush twitched, almost imperceptibly.

His eyes now widened in amazement; his sword drooped and then fell to the ground. The feathers of an arrow protruded under his arm, its point buried deep within his chest cavity.

King Strongbow stood upon his platform, a hundred yards away, another arrow already pulled back.

The multitudes grew quiet.

Rush swayed. He seemed confused. His questioning look first went to Fergus and then down at his chest. "I cannot die. You were supposed to die. I ... will ... recover yet."

Fergus stood before him, pitying him, knowing that he would not likely live much longer.

"Don't look like that ... I ... am only wounded." His voice was getting weaker; a tear rolled down his cheek; he swayed the other way.

"Make your peace with God, Rush."

"No ... why?" His head tilted with each breath.

"God looked down from heaven upon the children of men," Fergus began, his voice was kind, imploring, "to see if there were any that did understand, that did seek God. Every one of them is gone back: they are altogether become filthy; there is none that doeth good, no, not one. All our righteousness' are as filthy rags; and we all do fade as a leaf; and our iniquities, like the wind, have taken us away. The wicked shall be turned into hell, neither shall their fire be quenched."

Rush wheezed, "I am ... undone then."

"Listen, Rush. It is of the Lord's mercies that we are not consumed, because his compassions fail not. They are new every morning. The Lord is good unto them that wait for him, to the soul that seeks Him. It is good that a man should both hope and quietly wait for the salvation of the Lord."

"It's hard ... to ... breathe." No longer did Rush look menacing. He seemed a scared little boy. He tried to lower his sword arm, but the arrow was in the way and he gasped in pain, staggering.

Fergus stepped forward, held his arm aloft, and steadied him.

"I am so ... wicked ... is it not ... too late ... for ... me? Will ... He hear me now?" Rush was breathing heavily, sucking for air as if there was not enough to be had.

"It is not too late for God's mercies, but you must cry out to Him for that mercy. Every man is a sinner, but blessed is that man whose sins are not imputed to him. He that covers his sins shall not prosper: but whoso confesses and forsakes them shall have mercy." Fergus could feel Rush's weight bearing upon his arms; Rush's legs began to tremble.

"Don't let me fall … don't lay me down … please … I cannot die while I yet stand."

"Listen, there is a heaven to attain and a hell to run from. Come now, and let us reason together, saith the LORD: though your sins be as scarlet, they shall be as white as snow; though they be red like crimson, they shall be as wool. Will you trust in the god hanging about your neck, or the one true God, for your salvation?"

"I … am … afraid." These words were less than whispers.

The king's voice echoed through the silent arena. "Let him go!"

Rush's eyes rose in fear. But there was no more strength in him to speak.

"Shall I remove the idol about your neck?"

The movement was ever so slight. Yet Fergus was sure that Rush had nodded his head.

Fergus, holding him up with one arm, snapped the idol free and threw it to the ground. Rush's legs buckled, but Fergus lifted him back to his feet before he could fall. No longer could he hold him at arms length. Careful not to bump the arrow, Fergus hugged Rush to his own body, and continued to tell him of God's love and mercy.

Rush shuddered and exhaled. It almost sounded as if he said something, but what it was Fergus could not tell.

Rush took one more ragged breath; it was his last.

Fergus laid him gently to the ground; he cradled his head. "I hope we meet again, my friend. Precious in the sight of the Lord is the death of His saints."

The Master of Games cleared his throat. "The king wishes to see you."

Gimcrack's Search

Gimcrack had been gathering information all day, trying to find clues that would lead him to Staffsmitten. It was the Dragon Priests who had taken him from the grave-yard ... the Dragon Priests ... the very men he had purposed to never see again, and now he was actually seeking them out.

People's tongues were loose, as the fair and the games ignited their imaginations, but still, they seemed uncomfortable when the conversation came round to discussing the priests of the Dragon. No one knew where their temple was or would be built; no one knew where they were temporarily or permanently housed; but all had caught glimpses of them here and there, and all were intrigued by their presence, yet fearful too.

The last man he had queried—a shopkeeper—gave him a curious look, and then it seemed that he was the one investigating Gimcrack instead of the other way around; Gimcrack felt a pang of unease as he left the man standing in the doorway of his shop. The unease changed to an eye twitching anxiety when he turned to look back, and saw him still there, but now the shopkeeper was closing and locking the door. Suspicious. Yes, a very suspicious thing to do with so many potential customers streaming past.

Should he follow? It was possible that he might lead him to some information he needed, some clue at least. But now that it seemed possible that he might actually find a Dragon Priest lair, fear gripped his heart, and he found himself desiring the company of young Thiery. Not to put Thiery in any kind of danger, but the boy had a great ability with words, words about their God, words that truly refreshed poor Gimcrack and gave him a sort of courage that he had never experienced before.

Well, for now, he would just follow at a distance and make no rash decisions.

For almost an hour he followed the dubious-acting shopkeeper. He began to doubt whether or not the man was really up to anything when suddenly the shopkeeper stopped and looked behind him.

Gimcrack had begun to relax and therefore he had allowed himself to get too close. He froze where he stood, hoping the man wouldn't look directly at him. Yet everyone around them was moving. If everyone else was moving, and Gimcrack was the only one standing still, worse yet in the middle of the street, then it only stood to reason that Gimcrack would now be more noticeable. Try as he might though, he just couldn't get himself to move while the shopkeeper was looking in his direction, it was just too counterintuitive for Gimcrack's nervous constitution.

The fellow broke from the realm of suspicion into that of dark intrigue when he walked with obvious intent to the opposite side of the street and knocked upon a grand double door. What made the doors particularly suspect was that they did not enter into a home or place of business, but into a private courtyard, in fact, a private cemetery.

A shiver ran along Gimcrack's stout frame. Then, curiously, the shopkeeper looked down to the right of the door. Gimcrack followed with his eyes and saw a metal grate fixed in the cobblestones. The shopkeeper dropped something, covered it with his foot, and slid it toward the grate. A long finger poked up from between the iron bars and dragged the little object down below.

Gimcrack's mouth hung open, and a double shiver convulsed his shoulders and neck. A moment later, the doors swung open admitting the shopkeeper, swallowing him up, and then closing with a thump. Before it shut, Gimcrack saw the dreaded gravestones, sarcophagi, a marble statue of a dragon, but worse still, the flowing red robes of a Dragon Priest.

Before Gimcrack had time to faint or run away, a mob swelled like a wave and carried him further down the street. It was growing dark fast, and the closely crammed bodies towering above him further blocked the light. It was all he could do to keep his feet and not get trampled, when suddenly the wave stopped and spread out. The force that had both caused and now stopped the surging mob was a single man standing on a box.

A town crier with news of the day's proceedings had arrived.

He waited for the people to quiet. A bulbous-nosed woman next to Gimcrack elbowed him in his side. "Oh, thisy here one is a good one for the speechifying." She smiled at Gimcrack with black teeth. "We're in for a goody one." And then some others in the mob shushed her to silence.

The crier began what many said was his greatest oration ever. That is how Gimcrack learned of the combat of honor between Fergus and Rush. How the king had saved him, and how Fergus and Lady Mercy were compelled to sit through the rest of the games as the king's guests. How Lunace, Ogre, and Goblin had stood in the arena as the sundial moved for half an hour, waiting for opponents who would fight for their king and the land, for their honor; and of how no one was forthcoming. Not a soul.

"The giants strutted before us all," the town crier wailed, "wielding their giant weapons, swaggering with giant pride, and they mocked us by increasing the number of men they were willing to fight, trying to induce us to fight. Six men, seven men, eight men, a full score of men … and we hung our heads low … no one would fight." Here the town crier hung his head too.

The crowd followed suit with a moan.

"The news is more bleak than that, my friends. Who has not heard of the sad plight of Lady Mercy, niece of the king? Her plight with the Bachus priesthood, and her flight from the hunt, the death of her friends, and the duel today fought on her behalf. Bachus and the Queen of Heaven have petitioned the king for her death, and the king has partly submitted."

The crowd groaned, and some raised their fists in protest.

"I say partly, people of Hradcanny, for her death is not so certain. The Bachus High Priest has put forth a test. If anyone rises up to do battle with the giants and wins, then she lives, but if the giants win, then Mercy must die.

"But fear not, people of Hradcanny," the crier swung his own fist into the air. "For tomorrow the giants shall be met in battle."

The crowd lifted their heads again—a questioning murmur issued from some of their lips; from others a muted cheer.

"Yes, people of Hradcanny, met in battle by heroes. By Oded the Bear, Ubaldo the Silent, Igi Forkbeard, Fergus Leatherhead, and a mysterious hero yet to be unveiled, and maybe more shall join their ranks for tomorrow's battle … the battle with the giants … the battle to save the maiden … the Lady Mercy."

A great cheer burst from the lips of the crowd.

Gimcrack was moved by the speech, but more by the news of Oded and Fergus than anything else; he smiled and thought about how excited little Suzie and Thiery would be. So they had finally found Oded, and would soon be reunited.

The woman with the black teeth poked Gimcrack in his ribs again. "Didn't I tell ya? Wasn't it just as I told ya?"

"It was a fine telling, missus," Gimcrack responded, "grandiloquently done!"

She rubbed her hands together, pleased with Gimcrack's enthusiasm. "And I'll tell ya what's more, as long as ya don't go blabbin' it to every mad man on the street."

"No, missus, I won't."

She leaned in. Her nose seemed bigger and rounder the closer she came. "One of them very heroes is right across the street there, just eatin' the food that'll be sustenance for his arms in that there battle. I saw him myself, I did. Go peek if you like, but don't go blabbin' my secret or the whole crazy band of these madcaps will be knockin' the doors down to get a look."

"Thank you, missus, it was very kind of you to share your secret. I will take a look." Gimcrack's heart began to beat with the anticipation of it. Just to think that he might bring them home this very night! He could see Suzie's big eyes now, so thankful and loving.

Opening the door to the eatery, Gimcrack was met with a jumble of delicious odors, quiet conversations, and a few turning heads. One of which was the unmistakable face of Oded.

He looked directly at Gimcrack, but there was not the slightest hint of recognition; then Oded turned around and continued to eat. Gimcrack knew that Oded was kind of slow, but the big man always had a smile for him, and he distinctly remembered Oded calling him by name on a few occasions and even discussing Gimcrack's maps with him. Could it be that he did not recognize him now?

Gimcrack happened to glance into a corner just as he took a step forward. It was a well-concealed booth, with wide wooden benches that climbed up and over the occupants like a rustic carriage in the street. There were red robed men sitting in there. Gimcrack could see their sleeves.

Gimcrack was terrified. If he moved further into the room, a simple turn of the head, and they would see him. They would surely remember the only dwarf from Count Rosencross' expedition—the one they had cozen sacrificed. Gimcrack couldn't move.

"Oded!" He whispered fiercely, but not loudly enough. It felt as if his voice would constrict and then he would not be able to speak at all. Flee, flee, flee, were his principal thoughts.

"Oded!" Gimcrack managed to call a bit louder, more like a whine.

Still Oded did not turn, but some of the other patrons did.

Gimcrack tried to smile at them, but what came out was his lippy, toothy, protruding sneer. He could tell by their reactions that something was wrong. "Oded!" Gimcrack shrieked. This time, everyone in the place stopped what they were doing and turned to look, everyone but Oded, who kept eating, almost as if he didn't hear anything.

Red hoods had extended out from within the corner booth; Gimcrack froze, relying upon his usual strategy, hoping they wouldn't see him if he didn't move. Two of them stood up, followed by two more, and still Gimcrack kept still. They were coming towards him; his mind started screaming again: Flee! Flee! Flee! When he was certain they had seen him, he finally found the ability to obey.

Someone was opening the door behind him. Perfect timing. Led by his protruding toothy face, he ran headlong into the arms of the men coming in—half a score more of red robed Dragon Priests. Their arms enveloped him, a gag was thrust into his mouth, and a bag slipped over his head.

Giants

The priests carried Gimcrack down the street; they turned, and almost immediately the sounds of the city became muffled. Had they brought him to the private cemetery into which the shopkeeper had entered? Were they going to bury him alive?

Poor Gimcrack groaned as he felt them descending a long flight of steps; the air became damp and heavy, and the sounds of the city disappeared entirely.

Oh God, don't let them bury me alive! Aghh ... I mean don't let them bury me dead! Aghh ... oh please don't let them bury me at all! Anything but that ... I mean, not anything ... help Lord, help! Help! Help!

And that is all Gimcrack could muster, a pitiful cry to his God. He repeated it over and over, for how long he did not know. So immersed was he in his wailing supplications that all else faded as if in a dream.

He was suddenly deposited upon what felt like a cot; the bag was removed and his arms were free once again. He was in a small underground cell cut from the rock; one wall was wet with dripping water; there were no windows, just a heavy door with a tiny hole near its top, too high for Gimcrack to see through.

Three city guards and a jailor were peering at him over a dim lamp. He clearly had been transferred to their keeping at some point along the way, but Gimcrack couldn't remember when. He was only too glad not to be seeing the dark hoods of the Dragon Priests before him.

"He's not much to look at." One of the guards offered.

"Nope, sure isn't"

"You sure we're supposed to …"

"Hush, not another word, you heard what we're supposed to do with him, and he's not to know a thing about it."

"Should we not bother feeding him then?"

"No, they said he could eat in the morning, just before … well, you know."

"Yea, poor guy."

Gimcrack's eyes shifted back and forth between the guards as they spoke, fear publicized in his every feature. The guards shut the door and walked down the corridor, taking the only light with them; a few slanting rays bounced through the meager opening in the door. Gimcrack held his breath, not wanting the last traces of light to go, and then they too disappeared.

So that's what it was to be. Something was going to happen to him tomorrow—after he ate—something terrible, and now he had all night to wrestle with what it might be.

Please, God, please let me have some light.

He waited a moment, hoping; there was no light. Mercifully, Gimcrack laid his head down and almost immediately fell asleep. He did not even finish the next prayer on his lips.

He woke to his cell door opening and the smell of food.

It was the jailor; he had a sheepish grin on his face—a strange thing it was, he almost seemed embarrassed. "I brought you a good cut of steak, can't give you a knife to eat it with, but wait till you see how tender it is, don't even need a knife ... and some potatoes ... greens ... and my wife's cider, it's even warm still."

"Thank you." Gimcrack was somewhat heartened despite his fears, and the man's agreeable manner helped put him at ease. Gimcrack was further soothed by the delicious food. "Ummm ... Yummm!"

"Yeah, I've got me a good wife, and a good cook too!"

"Mmm ... mmm ... mmm!"

"We're lookin' to get ourselves a place of our very own ... we've been savin'."

"Mmm .... good idea."

"I think I've found me a way to get the rest of what we need too."

Gimcrack answered with his mouth full, "You should sell your wife's food."

The jailor chuckled. Did he sound a bit nervous? "I got a quicker way ... I placed me a wager this morning."

Gimcrack was good at sniffing out nervous behavior, and now he could plainly smell it. His belly rolled and flipped, and his heart began to flutter; he lowered his spoon.

"Oh, no." The jailor looked genuinely concerned. "You eat up, you're gonna need all the strength you can get."

Gimcrack didn't like the sound of that; in fact, it had a damaging effect upon his appetite. "What for? What am I going to need my strength for?" Gimcrack's eye began to twitch again.

"I can't say what for. But everyone else thinks you'll be the first to go. If you can just be the last to go, me and my wife will win a handsome sum, couldn't you do that for us in light of this final meal, which she made special for you?"

"Final meal? The last to go? Go where? I don't feel so good."

"Of course ya don't. Who would in your predicament? I'm just askin' you to make the best of a bad situation. You know, make a show of things, but keep your distance, and let everyone else ... well, you know ... what was that? Someone's comin', don't say anything about this conversation we've had, good bye now, my wife and I'll always remember you as a friend and benefactor." The jailor closed the door behind him with a genial wave. It was dark again.

The door opened up again as soon as it had shut. The jailor peeked back in. "I almost forgot. The wife said I should leave you with this here candle, to make your stay more pleasant. Women-folk are always thinkin' like that, aren't they?"

Gimcrack stared at the long candle, its flame dancing as the door swung shut, and for a moment it almost sputtered out. He remembered his prayer from the night before, asking God for some light, and there it was, holding back the darkness. He thought about that candle, and realized if it had come last night when he so desperately wanted it, then he would have fallen asleep, and the candle would have burned to nothing before he even got to enjoy it. God knew better.

Gimcrack also remembered how God had helped him find the stone that led to his escape with Thiery and Suzie, when they were lost underground without any light at all. Gimcrack thanked God, and felt some peace.

I'm not very good at this stuff Lord, but I'll try to bring you glory through whatever it is that lays in store for me today, please help me. And this feels awfully strange to say, but thank you, even for me being in this cell.

The candle had burned more than half way down when Gimcrack heard voices; they stopped outside his cell, now whispering. After a few minutes, with Gimcrack beginning to shake in wonder at what would happen next, the door swung open to reveal the three guards from yesterday. They too smiled. The jailor was not among them.

"We've come for you," The first said.

"Yeah, we've got to blind you again, but we don't have to gag you this time," said the second.

"And we consider it our duty to give you some encouragement, friend," said the third.

Gimcrack had never been placed in a dungeon before, but nothing was adding up to what he had expected. He was captured and sent here by Dragon Priests; now they most likely knew who he was, and that he had been cozen sacrificed by them before, and so it made sense that they would finish him off. In fact, it seemed that something ominous was planned for his near future. But while he had expected bread and water, or worse, he had been given a fine meal indeed. Where he had expected rough or indifferent treatment from his jailors, they had been friendly instead. He had to admit that it would be nice to be encouraged. He smiled feebly at them as they placed the bag over his head and led him through the subterranean passages.

"That's right, friend," one of them offered, "it's not so bad. When you find yourself in ... um ... how do I say it without telling you what I'm not supposed to say? Well, when all's ready, you just go in there bold like, take up your arms and start swingin'. We all think it's your only chance. Nobody will expect you to be the first one to the attack; they might even sing a song about you after you're ..."

The guard's sentence hung unfinished, so Gimcrack gulped, and finished it for him, "After I'm dead, you mean?"

"Oh ... well that's a strong way of putting things, and you never know—"

"Exactly right," interrupted one of the other two, "you might surprise everyone."

Gimcrack gulped again, "The God of Noah might save me." He cringed a little after he said it, sensing that these men were not followers of the one true God, and that they might stop treating him well when they knew that Gimcrack was. It was a cowardly way to think and he knew it, and so he cried out to God to tell Him he was sorry and asked Him to make him brave.

Nobody said anything. Minutes passed and still nobody said anything.

Gimcrack felt the pressure to say something that the guards would like to hear; he could hear his last words echoing in his mind, and he wondered what the guards were thinking. Then he felt the pressure to bring glory to God as he had told Him that he would, just that morning.

Gimcrack took a deep breath, his hands were shaking, but he realized that his eye was not twitching. "Noah's God saved me, and I love Him!" He had meant to say it quietly, but his nerves and shuddering breath forced it out of him louder than he expected, even surprising himself with its forceful sound.

Suddenly, the bag was plucked from his head.

Gimcrack had his toothy, lippy grin waiting for them.

The guards were not grinning back, neither was the Dragon Priest who was standing in the corner. His grimace was made the more ugly by the blue tattoos snaking about his face and head. There were other men here, too: more guards, some slaves or workers standing at levers and pulleys and various pieces of machinery. The damp was gone.

The chamber was large with a wood plank floor and ceiling and many doors and passages exiting from it. Along each wall was a cage with a winch, ropes, and pulleys attached to it so that it could be pulled up into the air, and perhaps even through the ceiling. It was hard to tell at a glance. There were also two similar set ups that were platforms only.

Gimcrack was standing next to one of these; there was a long stone sarcophagus upon it; no lid. Gimcrack rose up on his toes, and breathed a sigh when he saw that it was empty.

The guards brought Gimcrack to the other platform and handed him a battle-axe and shield. The men at the winch began to turn its wooden wheel and the platform began to rise with the slightest creak.

One of his guards spoke as Gimcrack came up level with the tall man's face, "Let's see what your God will do, then." The platform kept rising, and Gimcrack was soon elevated far above the chamber. A trap door above him swung open, fresh air and light surged in.

Gimcrack crouched, raised his shield, and gripped his battle-axe tightly. He knew where he was now, and that there could only be trouble up there. He didn't wait for the platform to fully rise before he dove away from the trap door and whatever might be behind it; he rolled and came quickly to his feet. The trap door slammed shut, and he was alone upon the arena floor—yes, a quick glance around showed him that he was indeed alone. But, up in the balconies and along each tier's benches was a sea of faces, thousands of faces, hushed and expectant, watching Gimcrack—all those eyes watching Gimcrack.

He found it hard to swallow. Was something going to rise up from below and come after him? He tried to recall if the cages were all empty, or if he had heard the sound of some beast before they sent him up to the arena floor. Then he thought of the other entrances ... he turned, his foot scraped lightly on the wood, and he looked to the first portcullis on his right.

Giants, three of them. They look eager, but their gate does not rise.

Gimcrack turns, turns again, scraping his foot; he looks to the second portcullis. Two huge men, sons of Giants. It's Oded! But there are two of him ... two Odeds! One of the Odeds raises a hand and waves, smiling. The other does nothing. Their gate does not open either.

Gimcrack continues to turn; he tries to make sense of what he is seeing, but he can't think clearly and he desperately wants to see what is waiting behind the other entrances. He turns. The third portcullis: Fergus Leatherhead and a man he does not know, but an able looking warrior.

Behind the final portcullis stands the powerful Igi Fork-beard. None of the gates rise, and Gimcrack wonders if he is to join in their battle or if he is to be part of some show just prior to it. Then Gimcrack hears a slight creaking of ropes pulled taut, and he recognizes the sound of the winch somewhere below him, turning.

His heart begins to beat wildly. A trap door opens. Gim-crack runs behind it, waiting to surprise who or whatever comes up after him. If it is a beast then he will fling himself upon the creature the second it rises into view.

Slowly the ropes continue to creak, and from somewhere below, he hears singing.

Slowly the platform rises, and then stops. Gimcrack peers around the open trap door and sees the stone sarco-phagus. A hand reaches out from inside and grasps the edge. Another hand raises a sword to the sky. Whoever it is lies still for a moment, and then speaks, "It's a sky like this that puts you in awe of your Creator."

Just as the man pulls himself to a sitting position, his back to Gimcrack, the four portcullises of the Arena begin their ascent.

Dragons and Dinosaurs

BILL COOPER:
(After the Flood, pg. 131)

"If the earth is as young as our forebears thought and as the creation model of origins predicts, then evidence will be found which tells us that, in the recent past, dinosaurs and man have co-existed. There is, in fact, good evidence to suggest that they still co-exist, and this is directly contrary to the evolutionary model which teaches that dinosaurs lived millions of years before man came along, and that no man therefore can ever have seen a living dinosaur. And to test that assertion, we will now examine the issue by considering the written evidence that has survived from the records of various ancient peoples that describe, sometimes in the most graphic detail, human encounters with living giant reptiles that we would call dinosaurs. And as we shall see, some of those records are not so ancient."

I highly recommend *After the Flood* for further study. It is one of my favorite books, incredibly exciting as a non-fiction read, and superbly faith-building. "Wow, wow, and wow!" were my constant exclamations as I read it, even the second time through.

It completely blows my mind when I look at the incredible fossils of huge creatures which we now call dinosaurs (a word that was invented by Sir Richard Owens in 1841, meaning terrible lizard) and compare them to the ancient descriptions from the book of Job. These passages call for more exclamations of Wow!

LEVIATHAN:

Job 41

Canst thou draw out leviathan with an hook? or his tongue with a cord which thou lettest down?

Canst thou put an hook into his nose? or bore his jaw through with a thorn?

Will he make many supplications unto thee? will he speak soft words unto thee?

Will he make a covenant with thee? wilt thou take him for a servant for ever?

Wilt thou play with him as with a bird? or wilt thou bind him for thy maidens?

Shall the companions make a banquet of him? shall they part him among the merchants?

Canst thou fill his skin with barbed irons? or his head with fish spears?

Lay thine hand upon him, remember the battle, do no more.

Behold, the hope of him is in vain: shall not one be cast down even at the sight of him?

None is so fierce that dare stir him up: who then is able to stand before me?

Who hath prevented me, that I should repay him? whatsoever is under the whole heaven is mine.

I will not conceal his parts, nor his power, nor his comely proportion.

Who can discover the face of his garment? or who can come to him with his double bridle?

Who can open the doors of his face? his teeth are terrible round about.

His scales are his pride, shut up together as with a close seal.

One is so near to another, that no air can come between them.

They are joined one to another, they stick together, that they cannot be sundered.

By his neesings a light doth shine, and his eyes are like the eyelids of the morning.

Out of his mouth go burning lamps, and sparks of fire leap out.

Out of his nostrils goeth smoke, as out of a seething pot or caldron.

His breath kindleth coals, and a flame goeth out of his mouth.

In his neck remaineth strength, and sorrow is turned into joy before him.

The flakes of his flesh are joined together: they are firm in themselves; they cannot be moved.

His heart is as firm as a stone; yea, as hard as a piece of the nether millstone.

When he raiseth up himself, the mighty are afraid: by reason of breakings they purify themselves.

The sword of him that layeth at him cannot hold: the spear, the dart, nor the habergeon.

He esteemeth iron as straw, and brass as rotten wood.

The arrow cannot make him flee: slingstones are turned with him into stubble.

Darts are counted as stubble: he laugheth at the shaking of a spear.

Sharp stones are under him: he spreadeth sharp pointed things upon the mire.

He maketh the deep to boil like a pot: he maketh the sea like a pot of ointment.

He maketh a path to shine after him; one would think the deep to be hoary.

Upon earth there is not his like, who is made without fear.

Psalms 104:25-26

So is this great and wide sea, wherein are things creeping innumerable, both small and great beasts.

There go the ships: there is that leviathan, whom thou hast made to play therein.

Isaiah 27:1

In that day the Lord with his sore and great and strong sword shall punish leviathan the piercing serpent, even leviathan that crooked serpent; and he shall slay the dragon that is in the sea.

BEHEMOTH:

Job 40:15-24

Behold now behemoth, which I made with thee; he eateth grass as an ox.

Lo now, his strength is in his loins, and his force is in the navel of his belly.

He moveth his tail like a cedar: the sinews of his stones are wrapped together.

His bones are as strong pieces of brass; his bones are like bars of iron.

He is the chief of the ways of God: he that made him can make his sword to approach unto him.

Surely the mountains bring him forth food, where all the beasts of the field play.

He lieth under the shady trees, in the covert of the reed, and fens.

The shady trees cover him with their shadow; the willows of the brook compass him about.

Behold, he drinketh up a river, and hasteth not: he trusteth that he can draw up Jordan into his mouth.

He taketh it with his eyes: his nose pierceth through snares.

Some Bibles claim that Behemoth is an elephant or hippo, what verse especially proves them wrong? _____

Look at verse 15. Could Job actually see Behemoth? _____
If Job lived after the flood, some time after 2348 B.C., then what does that say about dinosaurs, man, and the secular view that dinosaurs died out millions of years ago? _____

MORE DRAGONS:

Psalm 148:7-10

Praise the Lord from the earth, ye dragons, and all deeps:
Fire, and hail; snow, and vapour; stormy wind fulfilling his word:
Mountains, and all hills; fruitful trees, and all cedars:
Beasts, and all cattle; creeping things, and flying fowl:

Mountains, birds, and even dragons, can do what to God? _____

Isaiah 34:13 *(see also Malachi 1:3)*

And thorns shall come up in her palaces, nettles and brambles in the fortresses thereof: and it shall be an habitation of dragons, and a court for owls.

Jeremiah 51:34

Nebuchadrezzar the king of Babylon hath devoured me, he hath crushed me, he hath made me an empty vessel, he hath swallowed me up like a dragon, he hath filled his belly with my delicates, he hath cast me out.

Micah 1:8

Therefore I will wail and howl, I will go stripped and naked: I will make a wailing like the dragons, and mourning as the owls.

What is at least one of the sounds that dragons can make? _____

Giants

Study the following verses and I'm sure you'll be amazed, as I was, at just how much the Bible has to say about Giants. There are other scriptures, but this is most of them. Some of the fascinating tidbits that you'll learn are:

1) Scripture, at times, describes Giants as men.
2) Giants have children.
3) There were whole nations of Giants.
4) Giants were around at least from the time before the flood to the time of David.
5) There was great wickedness among at least some of these nations and therefore God allowed them to be destroyed.

You'll notice in book two of *The Peleg Chronicles* that three of the giants are named Lunace, Ogre and Goblin. Some of the words used in different cultures for giants have been: troll, ogre, and goblin. I was struck by the fact that King Og who was a remnant of the giants has a very similar name to that of Ogre, and that the giant Anak's descendents were know as the Anakims. So therefore, I gave two of my characters the names Ogre and Goblin so as to show possible etymological histories for the words.

Genesis 6:1-4

And it came to pass, when men began to multiply on the face of the earth, and daughters were born unto them,

That the sons of God saw the daughters of men that they were fair; and they took them wives of all which they chose.

And the Lord said, My spirit shall not always strive with man, for that he also is flesh: yet his days shall be an hundred and twenty years.

There were giants in the earth in those days; and also after that, when the sons of God came in unto the daughters of men, and they bare children to them, the same became mighty men which were of old, men of renown.

Numbers 13:32-33

And they brought up an evil report of the land which they had searched unto the children of Israel, saying, The land, through which we have gone to search it, is a land that eateth up the inhabitants thereof; and all the people that we saw in it are men of a great stature.

And there we saw the giants, the sons of Anak, which come of the giants: and we were in our own sight as grasshoppers, and so we were in their sight.

Deuteronomy 9:1-2, 4

Hear, O Israel: Thou art to pass over Jordan this day, to go in to possess nations greater and mightier than thyself, cities great and fenced up to heaven,

A people great and tall, the children of the Anakims, whom thou knowest, and of whom thou hast heard say, Who can stand before the children of Anak!

... but for the wickedness of these nations the Lord doth drive them out from before thee.

Joshua 15:13-14

And unto Caleb the son of Jephunneh he gave a part among the children of Judah, according to the commandment of the Lord to Joshua, even the city of Arba the father of Anak, which city is Hebron.

And Caleb drove thence the three sons of Anak, Sheshai, and Ahiman, and Talmai, the children of Anak.

Joshua 14:15

And the name of Hebron before was Kirjatharba; which Arba was a great man among the Anakims. And the land had rest from war.

Deuteronomy 2:10-11, 19-21

(Israelites passed by the way of the wilderness of Moab.)

The Emims dwelt therein in times past, a people great, and many, and tall, as the Anakims;

Which also were accounted giants, as the Anakims; but the Moabites call them Emims....

And when thou comest nigh over against the children of Ammon, distress them not, nor meddle with them: for I will not give thee of the land of the children of Ammon any possession; because I have given it unto the children of Lot for a possession.

(That also was accounted a land of giants: giants dwelt therein in old time; and the Ammonites call them Zamzummims;

A people great, and many, and tall, as the Anakims; but the Lord destroyed them before them; and they succeeded them, and dwelt in their stead:

Deuteronomy 3:11, 13

For only Og king of Bashan remained of the remnant of giants; behold his bedstead was a bedstead of iron; is it not in Rabbath of the children of Ammon? nine cubits was the length thereof, and four cubits the breadth of it, after the cubit of a man. *(Note: 9 cubits by 4 cubits equals approximately 13 feet by 6 feet.)*

And the rest of Gilead, and all Bashan, being the kingdom of Og, gave I unto the half tribe of Manasseh; all the region of Argob, with all Bashan, which was called the land of giants.

Joshua 11:21-22

And at that time came Joshua, and cut off the Anakims from the mountains, from Hebron, from Debir, from Anab, and from all the mountains of Judah, and from all the mountains of Israel: Joshua destroyed them utterly with their cities.

There was none of the Anakims left in the land of the children of Israel: only in Gaza, in Gath, and in Ashdod, there remained.

Joshua 15:8

And the border went up by the valley of the son of Hinnom unto the south side of the Jebusite; the same is Jerusalem: and the border went up to the top of the mountain that lieth before the valley of Hinnom westward, which is at the end of the valley of the giants northward:

Joshua 14:15
And Joshua answered them, If thou be a great people, then get thee up to the wood country, and cut down for thyself there in the land of the Perizzites and of the giants, if mount Ephraim be too narrow for thee.

1 Samuel 17:4
And there went out a champion out of the camp of the Philistines, named Goliath, of Gath, whose height was six cubits and a span. *(Note: approximately 9 feet 6 inches)*

2 Samuel 21:15-22
Moreover the Philistines had yet war again with Israel; and David went down, and his servants with him, and fought against the Philistines: and David waxed faint.

And Ishbibenob, which was of the sons of the giant, the weight of whose spear weighed three hundred shekels of brass in weight, he being girded with a new sword, thought to have slain David.

But Abishai the son of Zeruiah succoured him, and smote the Philistine, and killed him. Then the men of David sware unto him, saying, Thou shalt go no more out with us to battle, that thou quench not the light of Israel.

And it came to pass after this, that there was again a battle with the Philistines at Gob: then Sibbechai the Hushathite slew Saph, which was of the sons of the giant.

And there was again a battle in Gob with the Philistines, where Elhanan the son of Jaareoregim, a Bethlehemite, slew the brother of Goliath the Gittite, the staff of whose spear was like a weaver's beam.

And there was yet a battle in Gath, where was a man of great stature, that had on every hand six fingers, and on every foot six toes, four and twenty in number; and he also was born to the giant.

And when he defied Israel, Jonathan the son of Shimea the brother of David slew him.

These four were born to the giant in Gath, and fell by the hand of David, and by the hand of his servants.

Job 16:14

He breaketh me with breach upon breach, he runneth upon me like a giant.

Which one of the following is not a person or place of the giants? Ishbibenob, land of the giants, valley of the giants, Saph, Goliath, Anakims, Bashon, Jephunneh, Og, Zamzummims, Emims, Arba, Anak, Sheshai, Ahiman, Talmai, or Kirjatharba _____

Isn't it surprising how many giants are mentioned in scripture?